The New York Times

PUBLIC PROFILES

Donald J. Trump

THE NEW YORK TIMES EDITORIAL STAFF

Published in 2019 by New York Times Educational Publishing
in association with The Rosen Publishing Group, Inc.
29 East 21st Street, New York, NY 10010

First Edition

The New York Times
Alex Ward: Editorial Director, Book Development
Brenda Hutchings: Senior Photo Editor/Art Buyer
Phyllis Collazo: Photo Rights/Permissions Editor
Heidi Giovine: Administrative Manager

Rosen Publishing
Greg Tucker: Creative Director
Brian Garvey: Art Director
Megan Kellerman: Managing Editor
Danielle Weiner: Editor

Cataloging-in-Publication Data

Names: New York Times Company.
Title: Donald J. Trump / edited by the New York Times editorial staff.
Description: New York : The New York Times Educational Publishing, 2019. | Series: Public profiles | Includes glossary and index.
Identifiers: ISBN 9781642820195 (pbk.) | ISBN 9781642820171 (library bound) | ISBN 9781642820188 (ebook)
Subjects: LCSH: Trump, Donald, 1946—Juvenile literature. | Presidents—United States—Juvenile literature.
Classification: LCC E901.1.T78 D663 2019 | DDC 973.933092—dc23

Manufactured in the United States of America

On the cover: Donald Trump at Trump Tower on 5th Avenue in New York, NY; Damon Winter/The New York Times.

Contents

CHAPTER 3

The Transition

Introduction

DONALD J. TRUMP became the 45th President of the United States on January 20, 2017, after one of the most controversial campaigns in American history.

Trump entered the running as a political outsider and became the Republican candidate for the presidency. He took a strong, negative stance on immigration that sparked debate throughout the country. In his candidacy announcement on June 16, 2015, Trump referred to Mexicans as “drug dealers, criminals and rapists.” He also called for a ban on Muslims entering the country, a promise that he would implement in several executive orders later deemed unconstitutional.

Trump won the presidency not despite, but because of, his penchant for making inflammatory and divisive statements. When confronted with a fact-check, Trump would stand his ground often by attributing the information in question to an undisclosed “good source.” Although not all his statements were factually true, the manner in which he defended his words and said what other politicians would not say earned him the trust of voters.

Trump won the 2016 presidential election with 304 electoral votes, although he lost the popular vote to Hillary Clinton by almost three million. Trump’s victory was an eye-opener for many liberals, reporters, political pundits and the so-called educated elite. At the start of the presidential race, media outlets disproportionately covered Trump and his campaign. Targeted ads and fake news circulations on social media platforms such as Facebook also influenced voters, shining a spotlight on the dangerous potential of data mining and cyber warfare. The news coverage functioned as free advertising for Trump, who was an already well-known public figure before his candidacy.

TY WRIGHT FOR THE NEW YORK TIMES

Donald Trump at a 2016 campaign rally in Charleston, W.Va.

Before his bid for president, Trump's reputation was as a business and real estate developer and starring as himself on the television program, "The Apprentice." He attended the Wharton School at the University of Pennsylvania. In 1972, he became the owner of his father's company, Elizabeth Trump & Son, and renamed it The Trump Organization. Trump found his first big success with the opening of the Grand Hyatt Hotel in midtown Manhattan. His other high-profile addresses include Trump Tower, 40 Wall Street and Trump Place. His failed projects, many of which filed for bankruptcy, include Trump Casinos, Trump Airlines and Trump University.

Many organizations that had ties to Trump before his campaign were quick to distance themselves from the presidential candidate. Trump co-owned the Miss Universe pageant with NBC from 1996 to 2015. On June 29, 2015, NBC Universal ended its business relationship with Trump, citing "respect and dignity for all people" as a cornerstone of their values.

Although Trump was endorsed by white supremacists and accused of sexual misconduct, his seemingly volatile campaign was ultimately successful because he reached an untapped voter base. His promises to shake things up in Washington and "drain the swamp" resonated with groups who felt the American government was failing them, particularly in social and economic matters. Donald Trump not only echoed the mindset of these groups, but he also captured support from Republicans, even as he was critical of them and inconsistent in his support of the G.O.P. His rhetoric and attitude demanded public attention. He gave a political voice to those who felt they had none.

CHAPTER 1

An American Businessman

Before he would become President of the United States, Donald J. Trump had a career as a real estate developer and reality television star. A look back at the media coverage of Donald Trump's real estate career hints at his future character as president — one that emphasizes grandeur and spectacle over stability. Trump filed for corporate bankruptcy several times, a move that he has branded as business acumen. In 2005, The Trump Organization launched Trump University, an institution meant to provide real estate training, but has since been revealed to be a scam.

Donald Trump, Real Estate Promoter, Builds Image as He Buys Buildings

BY JUDY KLEMESRUD | NOV. 1, 1976

HE IS TALL, lean and blond, with dazzling white teeth, and he looks ever so much like Robert Redford. He rides around town in a chauffeured silver Cadillac with his initials, DJT, on the plates. He dates slinky fashion models, belongs to the most elegant clubs and, at only 30 years of age, estimates that he is worth "more than $200 million."

Flair. It's one of Donald J. Trump's favorite words, and both he, his friends and his enemies use it when describing his way of life as well as his business style as New York's No. 1 real estate promoter of the middle 1970s.

“If a man has flair,” the energetic, outspoken Mr. Trump said the other day, “and is smart and somewhat conservative and has a taste for what people want, he’s bound to be successful in New York.”

Mr. Trump, who is president of the Brooklyn based Trump Organization, which owns and manages 22,000 apartments, currently has three imaginative Manhattan real estate projects in the works. And much to his delight, his brash, controversial style has prompted comparisons with his flamboyant idol, the late William Zeckendorf Sr., who actually developed projects as striking as those Mr. Trump is proposing.

The proposed projects are:

• A large Manhattan convention center over the Penn Central Transportation Company’s 34th Street yards. Mr. Trump, who acquired the development rights from the bankrupt railroad, has drawn up plans for a $90 million center, hoping it will replace the stalled convention center on the Hudson River from 43d to 47th Street.

• A 1,500-room Hyatt Regency hotel following the reconstruction of Penn Central’s Commodore Hotel near Grand Central Terminal. Last April, Mr. Trump received a controversial $4 million-a-year tax abatement from the city, the first of its kind, for his proposal to rebuild the aging hotel building.

• Construction of 14,500 federally subsidized apartments on the Penn Central’s 60th Street yards, to which Mr. Trump has acquired the development rights. The site is bounded by West 59th and West 72d Street, West End Avenue and the Hudson River.

“What makes Donald Trump so significant right now,” said one Manhattan real estate expert, “is that there is nobody else who is a private promoter on a major scale, trying to convince enterpreneurs to develop major pieces of property.”

Commenting on the Commodore Hotel deal, the expert said he thought Mr. Trump was “on the threshold of the greatest real estate coup of the last miserable three years; if it goes through, you could call him the William Zeckendorf of Bad Times.”

The other day, Mr. Trump, who says he is publicity shy, allowed a reporter to accompany him on what he described as a typical work day. It consisted mainly of visits to his "jobs," the term he uses for housing projects owned by the Trump Organization, which was founded by his 70-year-old father, Fred C. Trump, now the company's chairman.

The day began at 7:45 A.M., when Mr. Trump's chauffeur, Robert Utsey, a husky, gun-toting laid-off New York City policeman who doubles as a bodyguard, pulled the Cadillac up in front of the Phoenix apartment building, at 160 East 65th Street.

Mr. Trump, who lives in a three-bedroom penthouse apartment done mostly in beiges and browns and lots of chrome, was waiting in front of the building. He is 6 feet, 3 inches tall and weighs 190 pounds, and he was wearing a three-piece burgundy wool suit, matching patent-leather shoes, and a white shirt with the initials "DJT" sewn in burgundy thread on the cuffs.

Speaking occasionally on his car telephone to his secretary and his banker at Chase Manhattan, Mr. Trump directed his chauffeur to make stops at the 60th Street yards; the convention center site, a federally subsidized Trump housing project for the aged in East Orange, N.J., which he calls "our philanthropic endeavor;" a middle-income housing project on Staten Island; the flagship 4,000-unit Trump Village in Brooklyn; and several other older Trump-owned projects in Brooklyn that the company bought in recent years.

"That's one of the reasons for our success — while others were building over the last three or four years at 10 percent interest, we were buying, at 5-percent mortgages," Mr. Trump said. "And the units they produced in their new buildings were much smaller than the ones we were buying."

Although the Trumps have been building in New York City since 1923, the family has not gotten as much publicity as other real-estate developers because they did not enter the Manhattan market until three years ago.

"It was psychology," Mr. Trump explained. "My father knew Brooklyn very well, and he knew Queens very well. But now, that psychology is ended."

EMPLOYS 1,000 PEOPLE

One of the reasons for the current intense push in Manhattan, he said, is that the Trump Organization, with 15,000 of its 22,000 apartments situated in New York City (mostly in Brooklyn, Queens and Staten Island), has a stake in the future of the city.

The organization, which is made up of 60 partnerships and corporations, also owns apartment buildings in Washington, D.C., Maryland and Virginia and land in California and Las Vegas, and it employs about 1,000 people.

"New York is either going to get much better or much worse," Mr. Trump predicted, "and I think it will get much better. I'm not talking about the South Bronx. I don't know anything about the South Bronx.

"But in Manhattan, I feel a new convention center will be a turning point for the city. It will get rid of all that pornographic garbage in Times Square. Psychologically, I think if New York City gets a convention center, it will resurge and rejuvenate."

As he drove around the city, he exclaimed boyishly, "Look at that great building [at 56th Street and Madison Avenue]. It's available! There are a lot of good deals around right now."

What attracts him to the real estate business? "I love the architectural creativeness," he said. "For example, the Commodore Hotel is in one of the most important locations in the city, and its reconstruction will lead to a rebirth of that area.

"And I like the financial creativeness, too. There's a beauty in putting together a financial package that really works, whether it be through tax credits, or a mortgage financing arrangement, or a leaseback arrangement."

"Of course, the gamble is an exciting part, too," he said, grinning. "No matter how much you take out of it, you're talking about $100 million deals, where a 10-percent mistake is $10 million. But so far, I've never made a bad deal."

Donald Trump was in the headlines in 1973, when the Department of Justice brought suit in Federal Court against the Trump Organization, charging discrimination against blacks in apartment rentals. Mr. Trump denied the charges, and later signed an agreement to provide open-housing opportunities for minority groups.

"We never discriminated against blacks," Mr. Trump said angrily. "Five to 10 percent of our units are rented to blacks in the city. But we won't sign leases with welfare clients unless they have guaranteed income levels, because otherwise, everyone immediately starts leaving the building."

'HE HAS GREAT VISION'

Mr. Trump, a glib, nonstop talker, suddenly turned quiet when he stopped at the Trump Organization's headquarters, at 600 Avenue Z in Brooklyn, to consult with his father. Face to face, the son seemed affectionately intimidated by the older man.

"I gave Donald free rein," Fred C. Trump said in his office. "He has great vision, and everything he touches seems to turn to gold. As long as he has this great energy in abundance, I'm glad to let him do it."

"Energy is a word that frequently pops up in discussions about Donald Trump. Besides being a fast talker, he is a fast walker, a fast eater, a fast business dealer and gives the distinct impression of being an early candidate for a cardiac arrest. Some of this energy, he said proudly, could be attributed to the fact that, "never in my life have I had a glass of alcohol or a cigarette."

His father said that Donald was the only one of his five children (three sons, two daughters) who had shown any interest in the family real estate business.

Donald, who grew up in the Trump-built family home in Jamaica Estates, Queens, began learning the business when he was only 12. He continued helping his father make deals while a student at the Wharton School of Finance at the University of Pennsylvania, from which he graduated in 1968.

"Donald is the smartest person I know," his father said admiringly.

Fellow real estate executives in this very closely knit industry also say mostly nice things about Donald Trump, even when given the chance to speak off the record.

'THE JURY IS STILL OUT'

"He's a very adventurous young man, and we're all rooting for him," said Samuel J. Lefrak, of the Lefrak Organization. "He's bold, daring and swashbuckling. But in my opinion, the jury is still out."

Harry B. Helmsley of Helmsley-Spear Inc., said that although he had never had any dealings with Mr. Trump, he found him to be "very active around town: I just hope he can put his deals together."

Even Preston Robert Tisch, president of Loews Corporation, who is regarded as Mr. Trump's No. 1 critic in the city, spoke highly of the young promoter: "He's a very bright, capable real estate man."

Real-estate insiders say Mr. Tisch and Mr. Trump are at odds for two reasons — the Commodore Hotel tax abatement deal (Mr. Tisch's company owns hotels), and the 34th Street convention center site (Mr. Tisch was long associated with the rival 44th Street convention center site).

Criticism of Mr. Trump came mainly from mortgage bankers and others in the money end of the real-estate industry, all of whom requested anonymity.

"His deals are dramatic, but they haven't come into being," said one. "So far, the chief beneficiary of his creativity has been his public image."

Another money man called Mr. Trump "overrated" and "totally obnoxious," and said much of his influence had to do with the fact that he was an early financial supporter of both Governor Carey and Mayor Beame and had powerful lawyer (Roy M. Cohn) and powerful public relations man (Howard Rubinstein).

LUNCH AT '21' CLUB

Mr. Trump has been meeting the right people. During lunch at the "21" Club, the waiters were bowing and saying, "Hello Donald," and other lunchers, including Mr. Helmsley and assorted politicians, stopped by to say hello.

Mr. Trump took exactly one hour for lunch, during which he ate broiled filet of sole with no butter, drank ginger ale, and chatted with two men representing the National Jewish Hospital in Denver, which plans to name him their Man of the Year on Dec. 8 at a dinner in the Waldorf-Astoria Hotel.

"I'm not even Jewish, I'm Swedish," he said later. "Most people think my family is Jewish because we own so many buildings in Brooklyn. But I guess you don't have to be Jewish to win this award, because they told me a gentile won it one other year."

Mr. Trump spent a profitable afternoon, earning a $140,000 commission for about 20 minutes work selling part of a housing project for a friend. A witness to the negotiations said Mr. Trump was a hard-nosed broker, refusing to budge from his original terms of $1.4 million paid over a four-year period at 9 percent interest.

'EXTREMELY AGGRESSIVE'

The transaction took place at the architectural offices of Poor, Swanke, Hayden & Connell, at 400 Park Avenue, where Mr. Trump had gone to visit Der Scutt, the architect of his proposed $90-million convention center.

"Donald's very demanding," the pipe-puffing Mr. Scutt said when the promoter was out of the room. "He thinks nothing of calling me at 7 A.M. on a Sunday and saying, 'I've got an idea. See you in the office in 40 minutes.' And I always go."

When asked whether he thought Mr. Trump had any shortcomings, the architect replied: "He's extremely aggressive when he sells, maybe to the point of overselling. Like, he'll say the convention center is the biggest in the world, when it really isn't. He'll exaggerate for the purpose of making a sale."

The architect broke into a big smile. "That Donald," he said admiringly, "he could sell sand to the Arabs and refrigerators to the Eskimos."

Mr. Trump is single, with no plans of getting married in the near future, although he said he was seeing one woman — a fashion model — fairly regularly. "If I met the right woman, might get married," he said. "But right now. I have everything I want or need."

He said he liked to relax at night by taking a date to such clubs as El Morocco, Regine's, Le Club or Doubles, or attending Knicks or Rangers games in Madison Square Garden. (He has season tickets for both teams.)

Mr. Trump ended his "typical day by catching a plane to California, where he said he planned to wrap up a "multimillion dollar" land deal. He has been spending more and more of his time in the Los Angeles area lately, staying in a house that he owns, complete with swimming pool and tennis court, in Beverly Hills.

Is there any danger that Donald Trump will defect to the West Coast? "Some of the best deals I've made have been land deals in California," he said with a smile. "I've probably made $14 million there over the last two years. But my friends and enemies are all in New York City, so I'll probably stay here."

The Midas Touch, With Spin on It

BY TIMOTHY L. O'BRIEN AND ERIC DASH | SEPT. 8, 2004

WHEN DONALD J. TRUMP kicks off the second season of his hit reality television show "The Apprentice" this Thursday evening, reality may be in short supply.

In a business career long protected by the safety cushion of a multimillion-dollar inheritance from his father, Mr. Trump has completed some well-publicized successful projects, like Trump Tower at 5th Avenue and 56th Street in Manhattan. But he has also had repeated failures that pushed him to the edge of personal and corporate bankruptcy.

Within the next month or so, the Trump casinos are expected to file for bankruptcy protection. And Mr. Trump, a self-proclaimed billionaire "many times over," must pay $55 million to maintain a minority stake in a gambling franchise he once owned outright.

But none of this concerns Bill Rancic, last season's victorious apprentice and now an employee in Mr. Trump's real estate operation.

"I'm sure it will all work out with Mr. Trump," Mr. Rancic said in a telephone interview. "It always does."

Indeed.

For more than two decades, Mr. Trump has weathered personal and professional vicissitudes by combining an acute marketing sensibility with unvarnished chutzpah. As the P.T. Barnum of the business world, Mr. Trump is a showman who has emerged as television's most popular guru for aspiring entrepreneurs and has managed to burnish a gilded reputation.

"He's got a very fertile and creative imagination about how to spin issues, and he's brilliant at turning lemons into lemonade," said Alan Marcus, a business and political consultant who oversaw Mr. Trump's public relations from 1994 to 2000. "If I ever had a weak company that I wanted to make look strong, I'd hire Donald."

However mixed his record as an entrepreneur, Mr. Trump has retained center stage, Trump-watchers say, by deftly massaging the news media, distracting attention from his business setbacks and doing just about anything to keep himself in the spotlight.

"He's like a kid, and he's got that brash, narcissistic thing that works for him," said Liz Smith, doyenne of Manhattan's gossip columnists and a longtime chronicler of Mr. Trump's ups and downs. "He has enormous appeal to the masses because of that."

For his part, Mr. Trump explains his marketing prowess as something that comes naturally.

"If you asked Babe Ruth how he hit home runs, he was unable to tell you," Mr. Trump said in an interview. "I do things by instinct."

Consider how Mr. Trump has handled his most recent financial problems.

In February, with his casinos hemorrhaging cash and teetering on the edge of bankruptcy, Mr. Trump issued a news release announcing that brighter days lay ahead. He trumpeted a possible investment bank bailout of Trump Hotels and Casino Resorts as a "recapitalization plan" and pointed out that bankers, despite planning to force him aside as chief executive, retained global aspirations for the company. In July, as Trump Hotels reported ever-worsening financial results, Mr. Trump issued another news release saying that he planned to build a $300 million, 64-story hotel and condominium, the Trump International Hotel, in Las Vegas. Only a few newspapers analyzed the mounting financial problems of Mr. Trump's casinos the next day; many more ran upbeat articles about the proposed Las Vegas skyscraper.

Mr. Trump said he was not consciously aware of issuing the news about his Las Vegas project in tandem with a poor corporate earnings announcement.

"I think I'm lots less aware of things like that," he said. "But people found that Las Vegas story great, that's true."

When Trump Hotels disclosed in early August that it planned to file for Chapter 11 bankruptcy protection, effectively proclaiming that the company's shareholders were about to see their equity stakes evaporate, Mr. Trump announced another innovative product: a signature line of retro, 1980s-style power suits selling for $575 to $650.

Jeffrey Brody, president of Marcraft Apparel, the company manufacturing Mr. Trump's suits, said the prospect of corporate bankruptcy did not undermine the glow of the Trump name. "With Donald Trump, you get one day of bad press and then 20 good days," he said. "People can identify with someone who has been through ups and downs."

Mr. Trump's financial woes are not new. A decade ago, he was forced to sell off or lose control of prized assets in New York like the Plaza Hotel and the West Side rail yards because he had saddled his real estate holdings with more debt than they could bear. Although he stated he had never personally guaranteed any of that debt, it later turned out that he had — thereby exposing himself to the prospect of personal bankruptcy.

Mr. Trump narrowly avoided that fate in the mid-1990s by tapping into his father's fortune and by receiving a financial lifeline from banks that needed his participation to bail out his sagging real estate empire. But he emerged with a greatly diminished set of properties.

Even so, he penned a popular 1997 memoir, "Trump: The Art of the Comeback," that portrayed his meltdown as a resurrection.

When pressed to offer some insight into the alchemy of remaining at center stage, Mr. Trump attributes his longevity to two things: "No.1, you have to love what you're doing, and I love what I'm doing. And No.2, you can never, ever give up."

Mr. Trump's showcasing of his wealth is at the heart of his appeal. He has said that he is worth anywhere from $2 billion to $5 billion, and he is routinely described on television and in news accounts as a billionaire. Yet there is very little evidence to support that notion.

Mr. Trump's stake in his casino holdings was worth $34.5 million before his company said it intended to file for bankruptcy protection. Now the value of that stake is difficult to determine.

Another leg of Mr. Trump's apparent wealth, real estate, is impossible to assess accurately because it is privately held and Mr. Trump has never offered a complete public accounting of its value.

The largest portion of Mr. Trump's fortune, according to three people who have had direct knowledge of his holdings, apparently comes from his lucrative inheritance. These people estimated that Mr. Trump's wealth, presuming that it is not encumbered by heavy debt, may amount to about $200 million to $300 million. That is an enviably large sum of money by most people's standards but far short of the billionaire's club.

Mr. Trump said that because his assets were privately held he did not have to offer proof of their value.

"What my father left me is relatively small compared to what I've done," he said. "It's tiny compared to what I've done. I'm a billionaire many times over."

Mr. Trump has also made an art of calling all of his real estate holdings the biggest and the best, though his financial travails have left him in control of very few of them. He said questions about the worth of his real estate empire came from critics who were envious of what he had.

"They're all jealous people," he said. "They don't have the No.1 show on television."

But for every critic, Mr. Trump has many more acolytes. Even in his darkest days, he has rarely attracted much negative publicity, which some observers say is due to his marketing discipline and an unwavering ability to stay "on message."

"In his world he's not the most successful, he's not the richest, he doesn't have the most clout in the real estate world, but ever since he came out of Queens he successfully controlled the communications process," said John V. Allen, an admirer of Mr. Trump's marketing skills who serves as senior partner at Lippincott Mercer, a brand management consulting firm in New York. "He's very rarely defined by other people because he defines himself. He's out there talking so people have to respond to what he's saying."

Mr. Trump, of course, has never been shy about self-promotion. He has plastered his gold-plated name on real estate and casino holdings financed with other people's money, and his picture adorns Manhattan bus shelters and billboards advertising "The Apprentice." He offers nuggets of wisdom in best-selling business books, in 90-second radio commentaries and — beginning this month — in the pages of Trump World magazine.

On television, Mr. Trump pitches credit cards, telephone service and affordable women's clothing; on the tops of New York taxi cabs, his image endorses an employment Web site operated by Yahoo. He recently applied to the federal government for trademark protection for "Trump University," the name of an institution that will offer, according to the application, "online instruction in the fields of business and real estate." Mr. Trump even has his own brand of bottled water, Trump Ice.

As for free publicity, he will do just about anything to be sure people remember his name. In early April, he frolicked in a bright yellow polyester suit to promote a fictional restaurant, Trump's House of Wings, in a "Saturday Night Live" television skit. The following week, to drum up business at his Palm Springs casino, Mr. Trump matched wits with a chicken in a game of tic-tac-toe. (Mr. Trump won.)

While most marketing experts believe that too much exposure can be a bad thing, Mr. Trump has managed to make ubiquity a plus.

"He's consistent, he's simple to understand, and he's heavily marketed," Mr. Allen said. "He's never had to reinvent himself. Who he was in 1986 is who he is in 2004."

The Donald Trump of 2004 is a figure out of a fairy-tale world of his own creation. It is a universe defined by buildings outlined in marble, logos embossed with gold and blond girlfriends and wives with striking figures. And best of all, it is all open to view.

"He's one of the greatest choreographers of business and image that the business world has ever seen," said Peter Arnell, a New York advertising and marketing consultant. Like a handful of other business figures who have also captured the public's imagination, Mr. Trump has managed to "share his dreams in the public arena," Mr. Arnell said, which "allows for an infinite number of people to also revel in that dream."

That facet of his appeal is something Mr. Trump embraces fully. "I think sharing dreams is a positive thing," Mr. Trump said. "There is something crazy, hot, a phenomenon out there about me but I'm not sure I can define it and I'm not sure I want to."

"How do you think 'The Apprentice' would have done if I wasn't a part of it?" he asked before answering his own question. "There are a lot of imitators now and we'll see how they'll do, but I think they'll crash and burn."

Mr. Trump, through all of his business travails, has also displayed an estimable resilience. Jeffrey A. Sonnenfeld, an associate dean of the Yale School of Management, is a frequent critic of Mr. Trump's business practices, but lauds his durability.

"He doesn't retreat," Mr. Sonnenfeld said. "He doesn't acknowledge defeat in what would normally be considered a defeat.

"There is always a new quest," Mr. Sonnenfeld added, "that gets people excited about the future."

That sense of excitement has certainly greeted the second season of "The Apprentice." On the NBC Web site promoting the coming show, last season's contestants are asked to pick three words to describe Mr. Trump. Mr. Rancic said his mentor was "Smart. Driven. Likable."

Another aspiring mogul, Jessie Connors, offered a different assessment of Mr. Trump's talents. Her three-word description: "Smoke and mirrors."

New York Attorney General Is Investigating Trump's For-Profit School

BY MICHAEL BARBARO | MAY 19, 2011

THE NEW YORK STATE attorney general's office is investigating whether a for-profit school founded by Donald J. Trump, which charges students up to $35,000 a course, has engaged in illegal business practices, according to people briefed on the inquiry.

The investigation was prompted by about a dozen complaints concerning the Trump school that the attorney general, Eric T. Schneiderman, has found to be "credible" and "serious," these people said, speaking on the condition of anonymity because the investigation was not yet public.

The inquiry is part of a broader examination of the for-profit education industry by Mr. Schneiderman's office, which is opening investigations into at least five education companies that operate or have students in the state, according to the people speaking on the condition of anonymity.

The investigation is the latest problem for a six-year-old company, known until last year as Trump University, that already faces a string of consumer complaints, reprimands from state regulators and a lawsuit from dissatisfied former students.

George Sorial, a managing director of the Trump Organization, confirmed that the company had received a subpoena from the attorney general's office, and said, "We look forward to resolving this matter and intend to fully cooperate with their inquiry."

Mr. Schneiderman is looking into whether the schools and their recruiters misrepresent their ability to find students jobs, the quality of instruction, the cost of attending, and their programs accreditation, among other things. Such activities could constitute deceptive trade practices or fraud.

The four other companies are the Career Education Corporation, which runs the Sanford-Brown Institute, Briarcliffe College and American

InterContintental University; Corinthian Colleges, the parent company of Everest Institute, WyoTech and Heald Colleges; Lincoln Educational Services, the owner of Lincoln Technical and Lincoln Colleges Online; and Bridgepoint Education, the operator of Ashford University.

Spokesmen for Lincoln Educational Services, Bridgeport Education and Corinthian Colleges each said the companies had been sent requests for information by the attorney general's office and would comply with them.

A representative of Career Education Corporation declined to comment.

For-profit schools have become big business in the United States, especially as the unemployed seek a way back into the work force. Some of those schools, however, have been accused of creating as much economic harm as help: Students have reported falling deep into debt to pay for classes that they said had failed to deliver what they had promised.

Mr. Trump's institution is unique among for-profit schools: It is built almost entirely around the prestige and prominence of a single individual. Mr. Trump said he created the university in 2005 to impart decades' worth of his business acumen to the general public. He aggressively marketed the school, telling students that his handpicked instructors would "teach you better than the best business school," according to a transcript of a Web video.

The school has charged premium prices because of the Trump name, with the cost of the courses ranging from $1,500 to $35,000 each.

But, as The New York Times reported last week, dozens of students have complained about the quality of the program to the attorneys general of New York, Texas, Florida and Illinois. The Better Business Bureau gave the school a D-minus for 2010, its second-lowest grade, after receiving 23 complaints. Over the last three years, New York and Maryland have told the company to drop the word "university" from its title, saying that using it violated state education laws. (The school was renamed the Trump Entrepreneur Initiative in 2010.)

Four former students filed a suit against Trump University last year in a federal court in California, seeking class-action status. They contended that the school used high-pressure sales tactics to enroll students in the costly classes, promised extensive one-on-one instruction that did not materialize and employed "mentors" who at times recommended investments from which they stood to profit.

Mr. Sorial of the Trump Organization, which oversees Mr. Trump's businesses, forcefully disputed those claims. He said on Thursday that 95 percent of the school's students in New York had rated their courses as "excellent" on evaluation forms. The school's national average is even higher, he said.

"Our customer satisfaction surveys speak for themselves," he said.

As its troubles have mounted, the school has suspended new classes and begun overhauling its curriculum, executives said. One priority is finding a way to inject more of Mr. Trump into the program.

"The one thing is that they really wanted me involved, instead of the teachers," Mr. Trump said in an interview last week.

In interviews, several former students said they felt betrayed by the real estate mogul and his school, especially after investing tens of thousands of dollars in what they thought was to be a comprehensive education.

"They lure you in with false promises," said Patricia Murphy, 57, of the Bronx, who is among the former students suing Mr. Trump, whose suit makes similar claims. She said she had spent about $12,000 on Trump University classes, much of it paid with credit cards, in the hope of escaping her career as a part-time teacher and becoming a real estate investor.

Her instructors said they would introduce her to banks, help her secure loans and walk her, step by step, through deals, she recalled. "They did none of that," she said. "I was scammed."

Mr. Sorial said the school was looking into Ms. Murphy's claims.

Carmen Mendez, 59, a public school teacher in Brooklyn, wrote to the Better Business Bureau in 2009 about her disappointment with the school — and with Mr. Trump. She said she had dipped into her retirement savings to pay nearly $35,000 for the classes, because "Mr. Trump is a very respectable person, and I thought that Trump University was a real institution," she said in the letter to the Better Business Bureau.

An instructor promised her, she wrote, that the school guaranteed financial assistance to buy real estate. But once she had enrolled, Ms. Mendez wrote, she was refused such assistance. Because her credit cards were loaded with debt to pay for the classes, mortgage brokers told her she was ineligible for a loan, she said.

"I am writing because I want people to be aware that Trump University is not a real educational institution," she told the Better Business Bureau. "Please advise other people so they do not lose their savings in these difficult days."

Mr. Sorial said that the school tried to offer Ms. Mendez a full refund more than six months ago. "She failed to return our numerous calls and e-mails," he said.

Trump University's Checkered Past Haunting Candidate

BY STEPHANIE SAUL | FEB. 26, 2016

THE NOW-DEFUNCT Trump University, the subject of one of Marco Rubio's attacks on Donald J. Trump at the Republican presidential debate on Thursday night, was not a real university at all but a series of seminars held in hotels across the country that promised to share Mr. Trump's real estate investing acumen with students. It is still embroiled in lawsuits accusing it of misrepresentation.

Those who ultimately bought premium packages paid as much as $35,000 for the privilege of additional training, called mentorships and apprenticeships.

"Seventy-six percent of the world's millionaires made their fortunes in real estate," Mr. Trump said in an email marketing blast sent to tens of thousands of potential customers. "Now it's your turn. My father did it, I did it, and now I'm ready to teach you how to do it."

As many as 7,000 people across the country bought the sales pitch, spending an estimated $40 million. Both the State of New York and many of the students are now suing Mr. Trump for misrepresentation. Three cases are pending: one in New York brought by the attorney general and two in California, certified as class actions.

Defending the venture at the debate, Mr. Trump said, "They actually did a very good job, and I've won most of the lawsuits." The remark came after Mr. Rubio accused Trump University of being a fake school.

"There are people that borrowed $36,000 to go to Trump University, and they're suing him now," Mr. Rubio said. "And you know what they got? They got to take a picture with a cardboard cutout of Donald Trump."

In fact, the cases against Mr. Trump have not been resolved. One of those that remains pending was filed in 2013 by the New York State attorney general, Eric T. Schneiderman. It accuses Trump University of running a “bait and switch” scheme and said widely distributed advertisements for the program were replete with false claims.

One ad published at least 170 times across the country in 2009, according to Mr. Schneiderman’s office, promised that students would “learn from Donald Trump’s handpicked instructors, and that participants would have access to Trump’s real estate ‘secrets.’ ”

But an investigation by Mr. Schneiderman’s office found that Mr. Trump had little to do with picking instructors or developing the curriculums for the seminars, which were run largely by people with motivational speaking backgrounds who were compensated based on how many people they persuaded to buy additional seminars. One of them was a manager at a Buffalo Wild Wings.

Daniel Petrocelli, a lawyer representing Mr. Trump in the California cases, said Mr. Trump believes the allegations are false.

Mr. Petrocelli said participants in Trump University “were very happy with the courses.”

“They filled out surveys with extremely high ratings,” he said. “There was a refund policy, and those who asked for refunds received them. And, long after the fact, after taking these courses, some people want their money back.”

Trump University was founded in 2004 as an online operation, after a Rye, N.Y., businessman, Michael Sexton, approached Mr. Trump with the idea. After an initial investment by Mr. Trump of about $2 million, the business was based in the Trump Building, at 40 Wall Street in Manhattan. According to the attorney general’s office, the day-to-day operations were managed by the Trump Organization and its affiliates.

As early as 2005, the New York State Department of Education warned Trump University that it was operating an unlicensed educational institution in violation of state law, according to the investigation. In 2010, Trump University’s name was changed to the Trump Entrepreneur Initiative.

The marketing plan remained the same, however, beginning with a pitch to attend what was called a free 90-minute seminar to learn how to make money in real estate. In reality, the seminar was a sales pitch to attend a three-day seminar costing $1,495, the investigation found.

The instructors tried to persuade students to purchase the three-day seminar with unrealistic predictions of their success, the attorney general says. In some seminars, students were told that if they signed up for the three-day seminar, they could earn six-figure incomes within a year working five to seven hours a week. The speaker repeatedly implied that Mr. Trump would show up for the seminar, saying he "often drops by" and "might show up" and "you never know when he might show up."

Students were told they could go to the next level by signing up for the Elite mentorship and apprenticeship programs for additional costs of up to $35,000.

One woman from Schoharie, N.Y., who was caring for a son with Down syndrome, said she had attended the three-day program at a hotel in Malta, N.Y. The woman, Kathleen Meese, said she was told that she would make money faster if she signed up for the Gold Elite program, a mentorship, for $25,000.

When Ms. Meese said she had a credit card with a $30,000 limit but could not spend it on the program, she recounted, she was told by a Trump University trainer that "I had to find the resources to invest in my future." She was promised that she would make the money back within 60 days, she said.

But the mentorship involved visiting a few rental properties.

"I was unable to get my refund and am still paying off debts from my Trump tuition," Ms. Meese wrote in an affidavit in the attorney general's suit.

Seminar participants, she said, were told they would have their photos taken with Mr. Trump.

"It ended up being a cardboard cutout of Mr. Trump," she wrote.

Between Playboy's Pages, a Peek at How a Future Donald Trump Would Campaign

BY MICHAEL BARBARO | MARCH 31, 2016

BOOKENDED BY ADS for Trojan condoms and Malibu Ultra Light cigarettes, the lengthy interview in Playboy magazine is a remarkably prophetic document. Twenty-six years ago this month, Donald J. Trump sat down with Glenn Plaskin, a celebrity columnist, and, over a glass of chilled Coke, offered a grievance-filled economic agenda, a searing denunciation of weak-kneed American leadership and a keen understanding of his appeal to blue-collar Americans that uncannily resembled the White House campaign he is waging today — without Twitter, which didn't yet exist.

A glossy time capsule, the interview is testament to consistency, stubbornness or stuntedness, depending on your view.

Below are excerpts from the original interview, along with an analysis of how they stack up against his 2016 message.

ON WHICH AMERICANS WOULD SUPPORT A HYPOTHETICAL TRUMP BID FOR THE WHITE HOUSE:

1990 "The working guy would elect me. He likes me. When I walk down the street, those cabbies start yelling out their windows."

2016 The working guy is electing him, state after state, as he marches to the Republican nomination.

ON THE ASPIRATIONAL POWER OF HIS OSTENTATIOUS WEALTH — THE YACHT, TOWERS AND PLANES:

1990 "Props for the show .... The show is Trump, and it's sold-out performances everywhere. I've had fun doing it and will continue to have fun, and I think most people enjoy it."

2016 Now they are props for his campaign, signifying his financial success and voters' desire to replicate it. Mr. Trump's gold-plated 757 is a fixation of cable news, its landings and takeoffs chronicled live. And in Iowa, the real estate mogul offered free rides to children aboard his $7 million helicopter.

ON ALLIES TAKING ADVANTAGE OF AMERICA'S GENEROSITY:

1990 "We Americans are laughed at around the world for losing 150 billion dollars year after year, for defending wealthy nations for nothing, nations that would be wiped out in about 15 minutes if weren't for us. Our 'allies' are making billions screwing us."

2016 He makes precisely the same argument today, wondering why the United States adheres to costly "one-sided" defense agreements with nations like Japan and South Korea — and suggesting that they develop their own nuclear capabilities so America need not rush to their aid.

ON WHOM HE WOULD TRUST TO CARRY OUT HIS VISION IN GOVERNMENT:

1990 "I think if we had people from the business community — the Carl Icahns, the Ross Perots — negotiating some of our foreign policy, we'd have respect around the world."

2016 On this, Mr. Trump is strikingly consistent, right down to his mention of Mr. Icahn, a billionaire corporate raider, as an archetypal negotiator. Mr. Trump still names him as a future member of his cabinet.

ON THE LAMENESS OF PREVIOUS PRESIDENTS:

1990 "We're still suffering from a loss of respect that goes back to the Carter administration, when helicopters were crashing into one another in Iran. That was Carter's emblem. There he was, being carried off from a race, needing oxygen. I don't want my president to be carried off a racecourse. I don't want my president landing on Austrian soil and falling down the stairs of his airplane. Some of our presidents have been incredible jerk-offs. We need to be tough."

2016 In only slightly more polite terms, Mr. Trump makes the same case now: American leaders are "stupid" and "weak" (if better oxygenated), and the country desperately needs his no-nonsense, bruising style. A favorite line on the stump still echoes from 1990: "We gotta be tough."

ON HIS LUST FOR THE COUNTERPUNCH:

1990 "When somebody tries to sucker-punch me, when they're after my ass, I push back a hell of a lot harder than I was pushed in the first place. If somebody tries to push me around, he's going to pay a price. Those people don't come back for seconds. I don't like being pushed around or taken advantage of."

2016 This presciently summarized Mr. Trump's debate style throughout the 2016 campaign: Criticize me and I will pulverize you. Just ask "low-energy" Jeb Bush, "Little Marco" (better known as Senator Marco Rubio of Florida) and "Lyin' Ted" (Senator Ted Cruz of Texas), whose attempts to mock Mr. Trump drew his unyielding wrath.

ON THE LOYALTY HE SHOWS TO STAFF MEMBERS, AND THEY TO HIM:

1990 "I have had the same people working for me for years. Rarely does anybody leave me."

2016 That boast applies this year, to Mr. Trump's peril, in the case of his campaign manager, Corey Lewandowski, who has been charged with battery in Jupiter, Fla., accused of grabbing a reporter at a rally. Mr. Trump, saying he does not "discard people," is standing by Mr. Lewandowski.

ON WHAT IT WOULD TAKE TO MAKE HIM RUN FOR PRESIDENT:

1990 "I don't want to be president. I'm 100-percent sure. I'd change my mind only if I saw this country continue to go down the tubes."

2016 Apparently, it did.

CHAPTER 2

The 2016 Campaign

Donald Trump announced his bid for presidency on June 16, 2015. As a well-known reality star, he was not taken seriously by political pundits until it became clear he had amassed a large amount of voter support. Trump reached his supporters by positioning himself as a political outsider. He made strong, sensationalist statements in rallies throughout the country, and appealed to a largely white, male working-class constituency when other politicians did not. Trump's rallies were often sites of protests and violence.

Donald Trump Scraps the Usual Campaign Playbook, Including TV Ads

BY MAGGIE HABERMAN AND JONATHAN MARTIN | DEC. 24, 2015

DONALD J. TRUMP, the poll leader for the last five months in the Republican presidential race, is about to find out whether he has permanently changed the rules of politics, or if some of those old standards still linger.

His long-promised "next phase" defined by new spending, such as a wave of television commercials, has so far failed to materialize, week after week. His advisers have not revealed the existence of any pollsters on their staff or any advertising team. He has no real research operation to examine his own vulnerabilities or those of his opponents and, based on Federal Election Commission filings, little in the way of a voter contact operation to identify and turn out his supporters.

Regardless of how he fares in next year's state caucuses and primaries, Mr. Trump has established himself as a political force, pushing Republicans toward a bellicose brand of populism that will linger even if he is not their standard-bearer.

But he has conspicuously opted against spending in conventional ways that could fortify his lead or harm weak rivals, discarding the playbook that winning candidates have used for many decades.

"On any given day, Trump can dominate the news coverage of the entire race," said Craig Robinson, a former Republican Party of Iowa executive director who now publishes the Iowa Republican website. "I can see how such power might make a campaign think that they don't need to spend money on costly TV ads and direct mail."

This strategy has so far not stopped Mr. Trump, whose campaign message is that he is a winner and who has shown a talent for attacking his rivals in new and unusual ways, from drawing 30 percent to 40 percent in national polls. He will most likely enter the election year atop the Republican race.

But it may have left him less strong than he could be in Iowa, where Senator Ted Cruz of Texas has taken the lead, according to a Des Moines Register-Bloomberg Politics survey, and in crucial early states that vote immediately afterward, like New Hampshire and South Carolina. And it could make it harder for him to survive an Iowa loss.

Mr. Robinson said Mr. Trump had hurt himself in Iowa by not augmenting his news presence with a parallel effort to push his message through ads, mailers and phone banks. "Such an effort would have also inoculated him from attack," he said.

If Mr. Trump's team had researched Mr. Cruz's weaknesses, for example, then incorporated them in Mr. Trump's heavily covered speeches and ceaseless television appearances, as well as in paid advertising, he may have been able to pre-empt or at least slow the senator's rise there. Mr. Trump does not appear to have used a pollster to target his message or identify pockets of support, except for one survey early on.

“While leading in the polls for months and not spending any real money on advertising is novel, the Trump team needs to turn on the spending for a real advertising and turnout operation or prepare to lose Iowa and New Hampshire,” said Scott Reed, the top political strategist for the U.S. Chamber of Commerce.

Mr. Trump’s aides routinely point to the fact that he has led the polls while the person whose allies have spent the most, former Gov. Jeb Bush of Florida, is registering in the single digits.

Mr. Trump’s campaign manager, Corey Lewandowski, declined to discuss advertising strategy, but he said that the candidate had “unlimited resources and will use those to ensure his message on how to make America great again gets to as many voters as possible.”

In the past, Mr. Trump has questioned the wisdom and judgment of candidates who spent lavishly from their own pockets. He mused to Fortune magazine about the business acumen of Steve Forbes for spending so much of his own money on his own presidential efforts, and told friends in New York City he could not fathom why Michael R. Bloomberg, the three-term former mayor, had funded his own campaigns.

In 2000, when Mr. Trump was toying with a possible third-party presidential candidacy, he had a contract with the motivational speaker Tony Robbins to make $1 million for giving speeches at some of Mr. Robbins’s seminars. Fortune reported that Mr. Trump had engineered his political events so that he would give speeches in the same cities.

“It’s very possible that I could be the first presidential candidate to run and make money on it,” Mr. Trump told the magazine.

In the most recent period for which there are records, the third quarter of the year, Mr. Trump raised just under $4 million from donors. He contributed only $100,779 of his own money in that quarter, and has lent roughly $2 million since the start of the campaign.

But some of the money Mr. Trump’s campaign spends is on reimbursing him: His largest expense in the last filing period, $723,000, was on a company he owns, Tag Air, which controls the fleet of aircraft he uses to fly to all his events.

Mr. Lewandowski, the campaign manager, has said that the campaign had hired a Florida-based advertising firm. He added, almost proudly, that it was not a politically oriented company, in keeping with the outsider image that Mr. Trump presents. He also said that Mr. Trump was prepared to spend $100 million on a conventional television effort if needed. Then the campaign began considering other ad makers, including Rick Reed, who helped make the famous Swift Boat Veterans for Truth spots against the Democratic nominee John Kerry in the 2004 presidential campaign.

But still no Trump television ads have emerged.

Beyond spending just over $200,000 on a radio advertising buy last month, Mr. Trump has not made any television reservations. For a candidate fond of a deal, Mr. Trump's resistance to put down cash on commercials ahead of time could wind up costing him more than necessary.

By waiting, he has consigned himself to pay a higher rate if and when he does buy television time. Political advertising on broadcast and cable is substantially more expensive when it is bought at the last minute, even though candidates are charged lower rates than "super PACs."

What is more, the airwaves are considerably cluttered by now, with little available television time remaining. Under equal-time provisions, stations would have to find ways to accommodate him.

"Trump has already made history by pulling out to a large lead solely on the basis of free media coverage of his campaign," said the political consultant Roger Stone, who left the campaign in August but has remained a supporter of Mr. Trump.

But Mr. Stone cautioned that there was a difference between "persuasion" and "turnout," and that the power of advertising, mailing and old-fashioned phone calls should not be discounted. "I do think he's going to have to use some of the traditional tools to turn his voters out," he said.

Imagining Trump Going the Distance

BY JOHN HARWOOD | JAN. 13, 2016

THE TERM "Republican establishment" refers to people like Scott Reed. Those people have had a very confusing year.

Across four decades, Mr. Reed has worked for his generation's signature Republican leaders: Ronald Reagan, Jack Kemp, George Bush, Bob Dole. Now at the United States Chamber of Commerce, he's watching Donald J. Trump challenge everything he thought he knew about his party's nominating process.

Republicans elevate their "next in line" mainstream leader. Straight from reality television, Mr. Trump has vaulted past big-state governors and senators.

The party has traditionally valued ideological orthodoxy. With Mr. Trump's divergence from conservatives on health care, entitlement spending and the Iraq war, Mr. Reed said, "ideology is getting flushed down the toilet."

Most important, Mr. Trump has upended the strategic dynamics of recent Republican contests — the dynamics that have led people like Mr. Reed to predict his defeat.

"The key to being nominated has been to be the last man standing against a totally unacceptable candidate," Mr. Reed said.

By "totally unacceptable," he meant an ideologically zealous challenger who could excite a disaffected chunk of primary voters, but not a majority.

That's how Mr. Reed managed the successful bid by Mr. Dole, then Senate majority leader, for the 1996 Republican nomination. Next in line after losing the nomination eight years earlier, Mr. Dole confronted an array of rivals led by the fiery populist Patrick J. Buchanan

Mr. Dole beat Mr. Buchanan in Iowa, then lost to him in New Hampshire. When trailing candidates faded thereafter for lack of momentum or money — the typical post-New Hampshire pattern — Mr. Dole

STEPHEN CROWLEY/THE NEW YORK TIMES

Scott Reed, left, traveling with Bob Dole in 1996.

cruised to lopsided victories. Mr. Buchanan failed to capture 40 percent of the primary vote anywhere.

In 2016, that formula for stopping Mr. Trump may not work. The chunk of Republicans embracing an angry message, Mr. Reed said, "is two to three times its average size."

Consider the combined support for Mr. Trump, Senator Ted Cruz of Texas and the former neurosurgeon Ben Carson — all cast by conventional strategists for the "totally unacceptable" role. The three outsiders command two-thirds of Republican support nationally. "Establishment" favorites like Marco Rubio, Jeb Bush, Chris Christie and John R. Kasich remain political weaklings by comparison.

Currently, Mr. Cruz holds a small lead in Iowa, and Mr. Trump has a big one in New Hampshire and most everywhere else. One hope for their rivals: a long, destructive siege between the two that opens a path to victory for a third candidate, perhaps Mr. Rubio.

That hope fuels an intense competition to become the top "establishment" candidate in New Hampshire, even if that represents third place. No third-place New Hampshire finisher has won the Republican nomination.

But Mr. Reed has an increasing appreciation for Mr. Trump's political ability. For all of his rhetorical fireworks, he has driven home his simple vow to "make America great again."

Mr. Trump "is the most on-message candidate of this cycle, by a factor of 10," Mr. Reed said.

He believes that at least half of Iowa and New Hampshire voters haven't firmly made up their minds. That preserves an element of unpredictability three weeks before voting begins on Feb. 1 in Iowa.

Yet if Mr. Cruz holds his lead there, Mr. Reed sees the nomination race turning on Mr. Trump's response before New Hampshire votes on Feb. 9. The self-proclaimed "winner" will have lost. The broad national terrain of 2015 will become a narrow, one-week battlefield on which "you have to win every day."

"Can Donald handle losing," Mr. Reed asked, "or does he flame out?"

He considers Mr. Trump's resilience in recent weeks a positive sign. Under increasing pressure from Mr. Cruz, Mr. Trump seized the headlines again by simultaneously questioning the Canada-born senator's eligibility for the presidency and hitting Hillary Clinton over her husband's personal scandals.

His skills at political jiu jitsu "are remarkable," Mr. Reed concluded. For the first time, he now believes Mr. Trump can win the Republican nomination.

Donald Trump on Protester: 'I'd Like to Punch Him in the Face'

BY NICK CORASANITI AND MAGGIE HABERMAN | FEB. 23, 2016

LAS VEGAS — In his final rally on Monday before the Nevada caucuses, Donald J. Trump said he wanted to punch a protester, who had been ejected from the event, in the face.

On the eve of what could be Mr. Trump's third consecutive victory among a fractured Republican presidential field, the protester — the third one to interrupt him at the event and who Mr. Trump said had thrown punches at security guards — really drew the candidate's ire. As the man was being escorted away, Mr. Trump repeatedly told the crowd that he wished for the "old days," adding, "You know what they used to do to guys like that when they were in a place like this? They'd be carried out on a stretcher."

"I'd like to punch him in the face, I'll tell ya," Mr. Trump added.

Mr. Trump has faced criticism over his response to protesters before. After a Black Lives Matter demonstrator was pushed to the ground at one of his events in November, Mr. Trump said in an interview after the episode that "maybe he should have been roughed up," before later pulling back from his comments.

But on Monday night, he held nothing back, and the crowd of thousands met every one of his lines with whooping cheers.

Addressing another protester, a man holding a sign that read, "Veterans to Trump: End Hate Speech Against Muslims," Mr. Trump repeatedly said, "Get him the hell out," as the crowd booed the man's exit.

Meanwhile, Mr. Trump denounced Senator Ted Cruz, who earlier in the day fired his communications director for spreading a misleading video with subtitles purporting to show Senator Marco Rubio saying the Bible has few answers. Mr. Rubio, in fact, said the Bible has many answers.

Mr. Trump, who has amplified criticism of Mr. Cruz in the last week using his ability to draw media attention, called him a "liar" and said that it was the reason he lost evangelical voters in South Carolina.

"This guy is sick — there's something wrong with this guy," said Mr. Trump, a criticism that could be damaging for Mr. Cruz as the race heads into a string of Southern contests with conservative voters on March 1.

Mr. Trump did not limit his rough talk to protesters and his rivals on Monday. Referring to the Iranians who took 10 Navy sailors hostage in January, Mr. Trump said the leader of the Iranians was a "rough guy with a rough mouth — I'd like to smack the hell out of him."

He also repeatedly belittled Sgt. Bowe Bergdahl, the American soldier who was vilified by some as a deserter after his release by the Taliban in a prisoner swap in 2014. "I think they slapped him around pretty good," Mr. Trump said, referring to the soldier's time in captivity.

Pointing to his many victories in the presidential race, Mr. Trump said that he was winning the support of evangelicals over his rival Senator Ted Cruz of Texas because Mr. Cruz was a "liar" and evangelical voters "don't like liars."

"This guy is sick," Mr. Trump said of Mr. Cruz. "There's something wrong with this guy."

He also made sure to remind his supporters about the importance of "voting" — he said he hated the word "caucusing" — and told them that they should go into Tuesday night expecting a tie, to help energize them.

But he also issued a warning to them: "Don't make me have a miserable evening."

Mr. Trump, leading in the number of delegates and states won in the nominating contest, also turned his attention to the general election, saying he would be aggressive against Hillary Clinton and repeatedly raising the specter of her email scandal.

Riskiest Political Act of 2016? Protesting at Rallies for Donald Trump

BY ASHLEY PARKER | MARCH 10, 2016

WHEN KASHIYA NWANGUMA learned that Donald J. Trump would campaign in Louisville, Ky., where she is a student, she walked into a FedEx store and printed two colorful signs she had found online, depicting his head on a pig's body.

Then she steeled herself for what has become the most provocative and potentially dangerous recurring act committed by ordinary voters in the 2016 presidential cycle: protesting Mr. Trump inside one of his own rallies.

The moment that Ms. Nwanguma, 21, who is black, held up her signs, Trump supporters ripped them away and began shoving her, screaming racial slurs and calling her "leftist scum," she said in an interview.

EDMUND D. FOUNTAIN FOR THE NEW YORK TIMES

Protesters being ejected from a New Orleans event.

"Did I enjoy being treated like trash? No, not at all," she said.

At least she came away unharmed. The same could not be said for Rakeem Jones, 26, a protester who was punched in the face by a Trump supporter on Wednesday as law enforcement officers were leading him out of a campaign rally in Fayetteville, N.C.

"He deserved it," the assailant, John McGraw, told the television program "Inside Edition" after the confrontation, which was captured on video from several angles. "Next time, we might have to kill him."

Mr. McGraw was charged with assault and battery and disorderly conduct, and the authorities said they were also preparing to charge him with communicating a threat.

As Mr. Trump has unleashed the pent-up fury of economically displaced Americans, a much smaller but equally fervent movement has materialized in response, of people who are determined to shame Mr. Trump publicly, even if it means withstanding hostility, slurs, shouting or violence.

In recent weeks, the demonstrations have intensified, interrupting Mr. Trump time and again, breaking his train of thought and challenging his ability to command the room. "Can the protesters stop for a couple of seconds so we can talk?" he said after several interruptions in Orlando, Fla., on Saturday.

Such protests are hardly unique to the Trump campaign, but rarely have they been as frequent or as hostile, and few candidates have been as angry in response.

The rancor is so blatant that Mr. Trump was asked about it during the debate on Thursday night in Miami. He said he had not seen the violent episode in Fayetteville, and when asked if he was encouraging his supporters' fury, he said, "I hope not."

But he added that some of the protesters were "bad dudes" who were seeking confrontation. The "animosity is like I've never seen before," he told Chris Cuomo of CNN after the debate, "and I hope we can straighten it out."

The tensions between supporters and protesters lately seem to be mirrored by clashes between journalists and Mr. Trump's entourage. A Secret Service agent was seen on camera grabbing a photographer by the throat and throwing him to the ground last month during a protest. And on Tuesday night, in Jupiter, Fla., the Trump campaign manager, Corey Lewandowski, roughly yanked the arm of a Breitbart reporter as she tried to ask Mr. Trump about affirmative action, she and another reporter said. (A campaign spokeswoman disputed their account.)

Despite pre-event disclaimers urging peaceable conduct, Mr. Trump's tone often seems to encourage aggression. The candidate has berated security guards for not ejecting protesters quickly enough.

Last year, he suggested that a man wearing a Black Lives Matter shirt who was beaten and kicked may have deserved it. In February, as a protester was being removed from an event in Las Vegas, Mr. Trump said, "I'd like to punch him in the face." And in Fayetteville on Wednesday, as people kept interrupting him, Mr. Trump lamented the "good old days" when, he said, protesters would have been treated more harshly.

Indeed, the disruptions have become as much a fixture of Trump rallies as the chants to "build the wall" and promises to "make America great again" — so routine that aides prepare for them, the candidate anticipates them and his crowds are instructed in how to handle them.

"If a protester starts demonstrating in the area around you, please do not touch or harm the protester," begins a scripted message that precedes all Trump rallies. To quickly alert local law enforcement, the message continues, "please hold a rally sign over your head and start chanting: 'Trump! Trump! Trump!' "

A cat-and-mouse game precedes each Trump appearance. As audiences filter in through security checks, campaign aides scrutinize those in line, trying to spot groups of protesters by their matching shirts or other telling signs. People seen as likely disrupters are often ushered out before Mr. Trump ever takes the stage. People ejected from a rally in Concord, N.C., on Monday included a man in a shirt that read "Fascist Trump," and a group of men and women in black and white shirts who had linked arms.

TRAVIS DOVE FOR THE NEW YORK TIMES

Protesters being removed from an event for Donald J. Trump in Fayetteville, N.C. Mr. Trump recalled the "good old days" when protesters would have been treated more harshly.

Perhaps not coincidentally, Mr. Trump has lately started asking his supporters to raise their right hands and pledge their loyalty to him, creating tableaus that critics have likened to the salutes of followers of Hitler and Mussolini.

The response when a protest breaks out can seem almost biological.

Trump supporters typically begin shouting, pointing, jeering — and sometimes kicking or spitting — at the protester, surrounding the offender in a tight circle, like antibodies trying to isolate and expel an unwanted invader from the bloodstream.

In Louisville on March 1, Ms. Nwanguma was shocked by the reaction from Trump supporters, she said in an interview later. A video of the episode shows her clutching her cellphone and pinballing among outstretched, shoving hands. She said she was thinking, "Oh my God, this can't be happening," adding, "I didn't have any way to assign any names to my feelings."

Mr. Trump tries to turn the interruptions to his advantage, showcasing his large crowds and commanding presence, alternately shouting "Get 'em out of here" and "Be nice."

In Concord, he referred to demonstrators as "my friends" and showed flashes of compassion. "Are you O.K., honey? Don't fall," he said, when a protester seemed to stumble.

But six minutes into the event, when another man was led away, raising both middle fingers to the crowd in a show of defiance, Mr. Trump yelled, "Out, out, out!"

"He puts up the wrong finger and we're supposed to take it nowadays, folks," Mr. Trump said. "Pretty sad. Nasty, nasty people."

Still, something is enticing more and more protesters to brave the hostile response.

Maria Alcivar, 27, a student at Iowa State whose family is from Ecuador, helped organize four protests at Trump events in Iowa. At the first, outside a football tailgate party, she said her group's signs were ripped and people shouted.

Now, she said, she and other protesters take safety precautions, meeting in advance to discuss the layout of each venue and agreeing that everyone will leave as a group if one is asked to go.

Ms. Alcivar said she always felt nervous before protesting, fearful of being physically assaulted. But once she begins, she said, Mr. Trump no longer has control over her, or her message.

"Yes, I'm scared and nervous in the moment," she said. "But once I start chanting, I feel super powerful."

MAGGIE HABERMAN AND KITTY BENNETT CONTRIBUTED REPORTING.

G.O.P. Legislators Face New Pressure to Decide: Can They Get Behind Trump?

BY JENNIFER STEINHAUER | FEB. 29, 2016

WASHINGTON — The unraveling of a party hierarchy increasingly in the shadow of Donald J. Trump has shifted to Capitol Hill, where Republican members of Congress are beginning to split between those who could accept, even embrace, the billionaire as their nominee and those who have vowed, "Never Trump."

Rather than unify, Republicans are feeling increasing pressure to align themselves with traditional conservatism or ride the wave of resentment toward it that has led many voters Mr. Trump's way.

"I told Donald Trump, 'This isn't a campaign, this is a movement,' " Senator Jeff Sessions, Republican of Alabama, told a large crowd of supporters Sunday when he became the first senator to endorse the businessman.

But Senator Ben Sasse, the freshman Republican from Nebraska, countered on Facebook: "Please understand: I'm not an establishment Republican, and I will never support Hillary Clinton. I'm a movement conservative who was elected over the objections of the G.O.P. establishment. My current answer for who I would support in a hypothetical matchup between Mr. Trump and Mrs. Clinton is: Neither of them."

While many senators are waiting for the results of the primaries on Tuesday to endorse Mr. Trump, renounce him or reserve the right to remain silent, many are privately pondering which camp to join. There is no playbook for the choice they face. In the last half-century, no prospective Republican front-runner at this stage has been the object of such intraparty animus.

Some members say they are merely reflecting their constituents' views. "I come from an interesting rural county with a lot of Rust Belt

ZACH GIBSON/THE NEW YORK TIMES

On immigration, Senator Jeff Sessions has found himself aligned with Donald J. Trump.

union folks, and Donald Trump is truly resonating through western New York," said Representative Chris Collins, one of a handful of House Republicans who have endorsed the front-runner. "It starts first and foremost with the leader who is going to make our borders safe again, and some of the rhetoric, he realizes, he now has to moderate."

But other leading Republicans are saying a Trump nomination could hurt Republicans running for re-election in swing states. "We can't have a nominee be an albatross around the down-ballot races," Senator John Cornyn of Texas, the No. 2 Republican in the Senate, told CNN on Monday. "That's a concern of mine."

Democrats are already seizing on earlier comments that Republican lawmakers, including Speaker Paul D. Ryan of Wisconsin and Senator John McCain of Arizona, have made suggesting that they will support any nominee out of party loyalty.

Several Republican senators, led by Tim Scott of South Carolina, have enthusiastically endorsed Senator Marco Rubio of Florida, while House Republicans are more scattered in their choices. But regardless of their first choice, lawmakers are facing pressure to choose sides in what has become an almost moral quandary for Republicans: whether they can tolerate Mr. Trump as the de facto head of the party.

"Just as the burden is on the establishment to understand that Trump will likely be the nominee," said Newt Gingrich, the former House speaker and presidential candidate, "so is the burden on Trump to understand that establishment doesn't have to support him."

Mr. Sessions has never been a leader of a large faction on Capitol Hill, and indeed on Monday he seemed to back away slightly from his fulsome endorsement, urging Mr. Trump to denounce white supremacists after the billionaire businessman initially declined to criticize David Duke, the former Ku Klux Klan leader.

But in at least one important area, immigration, Mr. Sessions and Mr. Trump are closely aligned. The senator has made it almost a single-minded pursuit to thwart any overhaul of the nation's immigration laws that he deems "amnesty," and he served as a one-man wrecking crew in 2006, 2007 and 2013 when Congress pursued changes to immigration laws. That role alone has made him a power broker in an election cycle in which Mr. Trump has soared in part because of his anti-immigration statements.

More Republicans, like Senators Jeff Flake of Arizona and Lindsey Graham of South Carolina, have been vocal critics of Mr. Trump, and former Senator Tom Coburn of Oklahoma, a staunch fiscal conservative, added his voice on Monday.

"He simply lacks the character, skills and policy knowledge to turn his grandiose promises into reality," he said.

Mr. Coburn's replacement, Senator James Lankford, a former minister, is unlikely to back Mr. Trump, reflecting a possibly growing discomfort with the candidate among religious conservatives even as he so far has won a sizable share of evangelicals' votes.

"I think a lot of people in churches are starting to say, 'This guy doesn't reflect my values,' " said Tim Griffin, the lieutenant governor of Arkansas, which holds a primary on Tuesday with polls indicating a close race.

"I don't let my kids watch shows with cussing in them," he said. "I never thought that would include Donald Trump on C-Span."

Representative Mo Brooks, Republican of Alabama, has broken with Mr. Sessions and thrown his support behind Senator Ted Cruz of Texas for the presidential nomination. Mr. Brooks has largely made an economic argument, but has also said he objects to what he characterized as Mr. Trump's admitted history of adultery.

Some members, particularly those in tough re-election fights, are electing to stay vague and elliptical. When asked in a local radio interview Monday about Mr. Trump's initial reluctance to denounce Mr. Duke, Senator Ron Johnson, Republican of Wisconsin, said more than once that he "prays every night" that the Republican presidential nominee "is a person of integrity, intelligence, ideas and courage."

For other members, the balance of the Supreme Court remains a key issue, and on that logic alone they are resisting being too critical of the potential nominee, no matter his flaws.

"I'd rather be in our shoes than in Hillary Clinton's shoes any day of the week," Mr. Collins said.

Worried about the prospects of a negative Trump effect on some House races — even though gerrymandered districts make it exceedingly unlikely for Republicans to lose the House — Kevin McCarthy of California, the House majority leader, is advising members to focus on local issues and priorities in their respective districts.

"I don't think there is any pressure in the House," said Representative Thomas Massie, Republican of Kentucky, who had endorsed Senator Rand Paul of Kentucky. "I think as the winner emerges I think you will see my colleagues in the House starting to endorse the front-runner. But it will be motivated by a desire to get a seat on the bus."

Donald Trump's Message Resonates With White Supremacists

BY JONATHAN MAHLER | FEB. 29, 2016

UNTIL RECENTLY, Jared Taylor, long one of the country's most prominent white supremacists, had never supported a presidential candidate.

"There's been no one worth endorsing," he said in an interview. "I mean, for heaven's sake, was John McCain ever going to do anything useful as far as the legitimate interests of whites are concerned?"

But Mr. Taylor believes he has finally found someone who will: Donald J. Trump.

This year, Mr. Taylor's voice could be heard on robocalls to voters across Iowa and New Hampshire, urging them to support Mr. Trump. "We don't need Muslims," he said on the call. "We need smart, educated, white people who will assimilate to our culture."

DAMON WINTER/THE NEW YORK TIMES

Litter after a Trump event at Radford University in Virginia, shortly before the presidential primary.

Then came Sunday — a banner day for Mr. Trump in the eyes of white-power advocates.

In an early-morning social media post, Mr. Trump approvingly reposted on Twitter a quotation from Benito Mussolini ("It is better to live one day as a lion than 100 years as a sheep"). Then, in an interview on CNN, he refused to condemn the Ku Klux Klan or David Duke, its onetime grand wizard, after Mr. Duke declared his support for Mr. Trump.

"God bless this man," exulted the Daily Stormer, a white supremacist website.

After the CNN interview, Mr. Trump pointed to his disavowal of Mr. Duke's support two days earlier. In an appearance on NBC's "Today" show on Monday, he blamed a "very bad earpiece" for his equivocation. And a spokeswoman for Mr. Trump, Hope Hicks, said he broadly disavowed all white supremacist groups.

Mr. Duke took no umbrage. "I'll laugh it off — that's fine," he said in an interview on Fox News Radio on Monday evening. "Donald Trump: Do whatever you need to get elected."

Intentionally or not, Mr. Trump's remarks are resonating with — and mobilizing — white supremacists, many of whom have traditionally refrained from participating in the political process.

He has their support, whether he wants it or not.

"I've never met him, and I cannot read his mind any better than you can," said Mr. Taylor, 64, the Virginia-based founder of the New Century Foundation and editor of its website, American Renaissance. "But someone who wants to send home all illegal immigrants and at least temporarily ban Muslim immigration is acting in the interest of whites, whether consciously or not."

It is difficult to quantify the reach of the various white-supremacist websites that are championing Mr. Trump's cause. Mr. Taylor says American Renaissance attracts about 300,000 unique visitors a month. Another white-power site, Stormfront.org, claims to have the same number of registered users.

But however limited the practical implications of their support may be, the symbolic implications seem clear.

"You can't help who admires you, but when white supremacists start endorsing you for president, you ought to start asking why," said Richard Cohen, the president of the Southern Poverty Law Center, which tracks white-power groups.

Mr. Trump is not the first presidential candidate whose efforts to exploit a mood of mistrust and resentment across much of the electorate wound up energizing those in its most racialist corners. In the 1968 presidential race, Gov. George C. Wallace of Alabama, a champion of segregation, won five Southern states in part by appealing to racial fears in a campaign waged against the backdrop of urban riots across America. He was beaten by Richard M. Nixon, who made a subtler appeal to disaffected white voters.

More recently, in 1996, Patrick J. Buchanan assailed illegal immigration as an "invasion," referred to Mexicans as a group as "Jose," and elongated Justice Ruth Bader Ginsburg's name in a way that many critics took as anti-Semitic — saying he was using coded language to excite bigots without alienating mainstream voters.

Now, Mr. Trump is embarked on his own resentment-based campaign, and it is not limited to a single region: His commanding victories in the last three contests came in the Northeast, the South and the West.

Mr. Trump's support among white supremacists has been building from the day he announced his candidacy, when he characterized Mexican immigrants as "rapists."

Since then, Mr. Trump — or "the glorious leader," as one white-power writer is calling him — has only grown more popular with that constituency, which cheered his proposal to ban all Muslim immigration and his since-debunked claim to have seen "thousands and thousands of Muslims" celebrating the terrorist attacks of Sept. 11, 2001, in New Jersey.

Mr. Trump has amplified the messages of some white-power proponents himself: In January, he resent a Twitter message from a site called @WhiteGenocideTm. And he has done the same with statistics on black-on-white crime that were later shown to be false.

Nor was Mr. Trump's CNN interview on Sunday the first time he had been pressed to repudiate his white supremacist supporters.

In January, when Mr. Trump was questioned about the robocalls made on his behalf in Iowa by white supremacists, including Mr. Taylor, he said that he disapproved of the calls, but that his supporters were animated by a legitimate anger over the violent crimes being committed by "illegal immigrants."

Mr. Trump's failure to distance himself more sharply from white-power adherents has been minutely observed in online discussion forums.

The American Freedom Party, a white power group, has a daily hourlong podcast devoted to him. And Mr. Trump will be a frequent topic at American Renaissance's annual conference in May.

For people on the fringes of the American political right, Mr. Trump's campaign has held out the promise of a white-power resurgence.

"The march to victory will not be won by Donald Trump in 2016, but this could be the steppingstone we need to then radicalize millions of White working and middle class families to the call to truly begin a struggle for Faith, family and folk," Matthew Heimbach, co-founder of the Traditionalist Youth Network, wrote on the group's website in October.

The Parent-Child Discussion That So Many Dread: Donald Trump

BY SARAH LYALL | MARCH 10, 2016

IT WAS MORTIFYING enough when the Republican debate last week introduced the question of whether it was appropriate for one presidential candidate to accuse another of wetting his pants. But the final straw for Gary Goyette and Andrea Todd, who were watching at home in Sacramento with their 10-year-old son, was Donald J. Trump's jarring, out-of-left-field boast about his sexual endowment.

"We were just incredulous," Ms. Todd said, when Mr. Trump leeringly declared that there was "no problem" with that part of his anatomy. She and her husband looked at each other, she said, and then looked at their son. "Gary said, 'Tommy, you've got to leave — you've got to get out of here.' And Tommy actually got up and ran out of the room."

Many unforeseeable things have happened so far in the raucous Republican presidential race. But the 2016 election — with its rudeness, crudeness, bluster and bullying — has also presented adults with an unexpected, unpleasant quandary: How on earth do they explain Donald Trump to children?

"Quite frankly, it's been quite embarrassing when I have an 11-year-old who is better behaved and more polite than some people who are the potential next leaders of our country," said Maury Peterson, who runs Parenting Journey, a nonprofit group in Somerville, Mass., that provides support for families. "This name-calling and making fun of people is basically the opposite of what he's been taught at home and at school."

Kathy Maher, a sixth-grade teacher in Newton, Mass., said that election years usually presented an excellent opportunity for students to observe the virtues of the American democratic process. But this year, she said, she worries about the school's mock-debate season, when someone will have to play Mr. Trump — a candidate who, if he were a student, would be sent straight to the principal's office.

Her school has a program encouraging students to speak up if they see someone being mistreated, Ms. Maher said, and for that reason, she has felt obliged to address the subject of Mr. Trump.

"I try really hard, when we discuss politics, to take a balanced view," she said. "But I felt I had to say something this time, because the things Donald Trump says wouldn't be tolerated in our schools. He bullies people, he name-calls, he makes fun of people because of their race, their ethnicity and the way they look."

What about students whose parents are Trump supporters? "I say, 'People might like some of the things that Donald Trump stands for, but there are better ways of saying it,' " Ms. Maher said. "I did say that some people like that he says things for shock value, like the crazy old uncle who just says whatever he wants. But as an educator, I can't support that. It's not funny — it's mean."

BRYAN ANSELM FOR THE NEW YORK TIMES

Jon and Zoraida Michaud with their sons, Thomas, 8, left, and Marcus, 13, at their home in Maplewood, N.J. Mr. Michaud said Thomas told him he was worried that Donald J. Trump would "bring racism back" if he were elected president.

For some children, Mr. Trump's message has filtered down in extremely upsetting, possibly dangerous, ways. Social media has buzzed with parents relaying their children's fears that they or their friends will be deported, walled in or walled out if Mr. Trump becomes president.

Jon Michaud of Maplewood, N.J., who is white and whose wife is Dominican, wrote on Facebook about a conversation he had with one of his two sons: "So if Donald Trump becomes president, he's going to bring racism back," he said his 8-year-old had told him. "That means Marcus, Mommy and I will be separated from you because we have darker skin than you do, right?"

Speaking on MSNBC's "Morning Joe" on Wednesday, Cokie Roberts put the question to the candidate himself. "There've been incidents of white children pointing to their darker-skinned classmates and saying, 'You'll be deported when Donald Trump is president,' " she said. "There've been incidents of white kids at basketball games holding up signs to teams which have Hispanic kids on them, saying, 'We're going to build a wall to keep you out.' "

"Are you proud of that?" Ms. Roberts asked. "Is that something you've done in American political and social discourse that you're proud of?"

Mr. Trump replied that he had no knowledge of such reports. "I think your question is a very nasty question," he said, "and I'm not proud of it because I didn't even hear of it, O.K.?"

As much as they might want to, parents and educators cannot keep their children insulated from news about Mr. Trump.

"He's omnipresent. It's going to come up, so you better be prepared," said Carolyn Lee, a substitute kindergarten teacher in the Hawaii public school system.

With very young children, she advised that parents remain calm and refrain from retaliatory anti-Trump name-calling. "Let's say the family's watching the news and they see this man on TV tossing water bottles and making fun of people," Ms. Lee said. "I would say something like, 'We try to treat people the way we would like to be treated, and somehow he's showing the exact opposite of that.' "

Richard Klin of Stone Ridge, N.Y., said he saw little point in trying to shield his 11-year-old daughter from the campaign. "I had this impulse to lock her away in an enchanted land where Donald Trump doesn't exist, but you can't," he said.

Mr. Klin said he had traumatic memories of watching his own father erupt into "paroxysms of rage" whenever he saw President Richard M. Nixon on television. "I didn't want to be that guy yelling at the TV, so I'm trying to cool it," he said.

In Los Angeles, Andy Behrman, a single parent of two girls, 8 and 10, said that his daughters continually accused Mr. Trump of violating "the double v's," a reference to their school's "virtues and values" program.

"They're not picking up on the innuendoes of his hands, they're not catching on to the genital issue," Mr. Behrman said. "But they're catching on to the fact that Trump, Rubio and Cruz are all talking at the same time, which they've learned doesn't make sense. It's not polite and it doesn't allow anyone to voice their own opinion."

Parents who support Mr. Trump disagree, of course. They say that his authenticity and his refusal to pander to his critics are more important than the words he uses. And they ask why America's children are so sensitive that they cannot be exposed to robust views, forcefully expressed.

"This is not about him being rude to people randomly," said Jeremy Diamond, a marketing executive who lives in Manhattan and has a son, 12, and a daughter, 15. "He shows passion and aggression, and that he's going to fight for his point of view."

Mr. Diamond said he was "confident in the integrity and behavior and values" of his children, both of whom have been impressed by Mr. Trump's take-no-prisoners approach, which Mr. Diamond called "strategic aggression."

"My son said, 'Daddy, he just wants to show that he is stronger than the other candidates and that he's not going to get pushed around,' " he said.

ANDREW RENNEISEN FOR THE NEW YORK TIMES

Ruth Ben-Ghiat and her 15-year-old daughter, Julia, at their home in Manhattan. Ms. Ben-Ghiat said the ubiquity of Mr. Trump provided a useful opportunity for children to examine their own preoccupations.

Ruth Ben-Ghiat, a professor of history and Italian studies at New York University, who has a 15-year-old daughter and has written about Mr. Trump for CNN.com, said for older children, it helped to place Mr. Trump in the context of a society driven by celebrity and social media. "My daughter asks: 'Why are you so obsessed with Trump? So what if he did a retweet?' " Ms. Ben-Ghiat said. "But we can tell our children that he's a product of our branding culture and our selfie culture and our attraction to reality-show television, where the behavior is so brutal."

The ubiquity of Mr. Trump, she said, provides a useful opportunity for children to examine their own preoccupations.

"They can learn to look beyond flash and glamour, to be skeptical of the power of messaging and branding, but also to learn that it's important that each one of us speak out and use our right to vote," Ms. Ben-Ghiat said. "And to listen to the other side even if you don't agree with them."

In Sacramento, though, Mr. Goyette and Ms. Todd have been unable to bring themselves to fully explain last week's debate to 10-year-old Tommy.

"He asked us later, 'What does it mean about the hands thing?' " Ms. Todd said. "But none of us wanted to tell him."

Donald Trump Borrows From Bernie Sanders's Playbook to Woo Democrats

BY ASHLEY PARKER AND JONATHAN MARTIN | MAY 17, 2016

DONALD J. TRUMP recently coined a dismissive nickname for Senator Bernie Sanders: "Crazy Bernie."

But that has not stopped Mr. Trump from borrowing lessons from Mr. Sanders — the Vermont senator whom he also frequently praises from the stump — on how to run against Hillary Clinton, his likely opponent in the presidential election.

On a range of issues, Mr. Trump seems to be taking a page from the Sanders playbook, expressing a willingness to increase the minimum wage, suggesting that the wealthy may pay higher taxes than under his original proposal, attacking Mrs. Clinton from the left on national security and Wall Street, and making clear that his opposition to free trade will be a centerpiece of his general election campaign.

As Mr. Trump lays the groundwork for his likely showdown with Mrs. Clinton, he is staking out a series of populist positions that could help him woo working-class Democrats in November. But in doing so, he is exacerbating the trepidation some Republicans already feel about his candidacy at a moment when the party typically rallies to its nominee.

Asked how Mr. Trump could reassure his own party, Senator Jeff Flake, Republican of Arizona, suggested the party standard-bearer needed something close to a complete overhaul. "He could start by saying, 'I was just kidding,' " Mr. Flake said, bemoaning what he called Mr. Trump's "protectionist" approach.

Yet Republicans hoping that their nominee-in-waiting will suddenly shed his brand of hard-edge nationalism to appeal to the party's mainline leaders will probably be disappointed. In an interview, Mr. Trump said that if he was president, the North American Free Trade Agreement "will be renegotiated and probably terminated."

Mr. Trump's approach has scrambled longstanding assumptions about how the two parties can position themselves in a general election fight, and could augur at least a short-term shift in how a Republican presidential nominee campaigns. Until Mr. Trump's successful campaign, unwavering support for free trade and the business community, a robust American presence in the world and a commitment to deep tax cuts have been articles of faith for the modern Republican Party.

But Mr. Trump, who has also made attacks on illegal immigrants central to his campaign while vowing to protect Social Security and Medicare, is plainly going to run as more of a Sanders-style populist than as a conservative. And this approach suggests that the 2016 campaign will not be decided in the increasingly diverse states that represent the face of a changing nation — Colorado, Florida, Nevada and Virginia — but in the more heavily white Rust Belt, where blaming trade deals for manufacturing job losses provided resonant themes for Mr. Trump and Mr. Sanders during the primaries there.

Mr. Trump recently offered a taste of his coming line of attack on the campaign trail in Oregon, where he praised Mr. Sanders for highlighting Mrs. Clinton's ties to the country's largest financial institutions. "She's totally controlled by Wall Street," Mr. Trump said, echoing a Sanders rallying cry.

Roger J. Stone Jr., a longtime adviser to Mr. Trump, said he expected the presumptive Republican nominee to grow aggressive on the banks. "Who's been tougher on bankers than Donald Trump?" asked Mr. Stone, suggesting Mr. Trump could appeal to some of Mr. Sanders's supporters. "He's taken them to the cleaners. I think he has a healthy skepticism and deep knowledge of bankers and how they operate. He's going to be tough on Wall Street." Mr. Trump has said that "the hedge fund guys are getting away with murder."

Mr. Stone added that Mr. Trump would also have a built-in layer of defense as he appeals to blue-collar voters, because he will be less vulnerable to traditional Democratic attacks over Republican efforts to rein in entitlement programs. "Unlike all these establishment Republicans, he's been adamant about never touching entitlements," Mr. Stone said. "You can't run that play on Donald Trump."

If by abandoning the traditional Republican playbook Mr. Trump were to put Michigan, Pennsylvania and Wisconsin in the Republican column, as some of his aides suggested, he would swing 46 electoral votes from states that have voted for Democratic presidential candidates since the 1980s.

"We lost two elections trying to do this by the traditional electoral map," said Senator Richard M. Burr of North Carolina, one of the Republican senators who has embraced Mr. Trump.

But for every voter Mr. Trump wins over with his ad hoc populism, he risks repelling others — including conservatives who are aghast at how, on some issues, he is trying to outflank Mrs. Clinton on the left. While he may put parts of the Midwest back into play, at least initially, his approach could also endanger his prospects in some states that usually lean Republican.

"I think he's more likely to take Michigan than he is to take Arizona," said Mr. Flake, whose state is home to a fast-growing Latino population.

The unease on the right with Mr. Trump's ideological positioning spans the party's factions, alarming national security hawks, fiscal conservatives focused chiefly on promoting free markets, and the Christian right.

And even when he has hit Mrs. Clinton from the left, he has also shown a flexibility that has positioned him on both sides of some issues. He has called for a higher minimum wage, for instance, but has also said the issue should be left to the states rather than have a federal increase. On foreign policy, too, his cautious approach to nation-building and intervention has been juxtaposed by bellicose remarks and a promise to be tougher on Iran and the Islamic State.

Representative Steve King, Republican of Iowa, said that questions about Mr. Trump's core beliefs were "a significant concern."

"He needs to articulate deeper convictions on the issues that matter so much to conservatives," said Mr. King, a hard-liner.

For others in the party, though, that moment has passed.

“He’s ceding Republicans who find his big-government approach antithetical to everything they believe in,” said Danielle Pletka, a senior vice president at the American Enterprise Institute. “He’s ceding Republicans who have long believed that America is a force for good in the world and needs to lead the world.”

In an interview, Mr. Trump rejected the notion he was shifting his appeal to Democrats. “The fact that I want strong trade deals doesn’t make me to the left of anybody,” he said. “I actually don’t think I’m to the left of Hillary Clinton.”

And the Clinton team, too, argues that Mr. Trump is out of step with Democratic voters.

“Donald Trump may try to make over his most dangerous and risky positions, but his opposition to the federal minimum wage, his tax cuts for businesses and the rich, and his reckless ideas on the use of nuclear weapons are all too big a risk to be in the Oval Office,” said Jesse Ferguson, a Clinton spokesman.

Two of the three pillars underpinning Mr. Trump’s campaign reflect his “America First” populist ethos: a broad opposition to free trade, where he says the nation is getting a bad deal, and a foreign policy that is muscular in tone but argues against nation-building and excessive foreign intervention. The third major plank of his candidacy, vocal opposition to an immigration overhaul and a promise to build a wall at the nation’s southern border, also puts him at odds with most establishment-aligned Republicans.

Similarly, by pledging to leave entitlements untouched as baby boomers near retirement — one of several major issues on which he differs with leading Republicans like Speaker Paul D. Ryan, who recently said he was not yet ready to support Mr. Trump — he is repositioning the party away from the market-oriented politics it has been identified with for decades.

But Mr. Trump, not even a registered Republican until four years ago, has little attachment to the party’s rightward slant.

“Don’t forget, this is called the Republican Party,” he said recently on ABC’s “This Week.” “It’s not called the Conservative Party.”

How Donald Trump Keeps Changing His Mind on Abortion, Torture and Banning Muslims

BY ALAN RAPPEPORT AND MAGGIE HABERMAN | JUNE 29, 2016

FLIP-FLOPS ON ISSUES can be kryptonite to presidential candidates. In 2004, President George W. Bush tagged the Democratic nominee, Senator John Kerry, as an equivocator with no core principles after Mr. Kerry inexplicably (but accurately) noted that he had actually voted for an Iraq war appropriation "before I voted against it." One particularly devastating ad showed Mr. Kerry windsurfing, reversing course with the breeze. He never recovered.

Donald J. Trump's own proposals have often been vague, his prepared statements often contradicted by his own off-the-cuff remarks

HILARY SWIFT FOR THE NEW YORK TIMES

Candidate Trump in Monessen, Pa. His proposals have often been vague, and he has reversed course on campaign issues, sometimes within hours.

in speeches and interviews. Yet he has so far avoided much harm, despite reversing himself — sometimes within hours — on hot-button campaign issues like immigration, abortion and economic policy.

Here, we count some of the ways Mr. Trump has vacillated.

THE MUSLIM BAN

Mr. Trump said in September that he was willing to let some Syrian refugees enter the United States despite the security risks. "Something has to be done," he said. "It's an unbelievable humanitarian problem."

In December, after the Islamic State-inspired attack in San Bernardino, Calif., Mr. Trump shocked even many Republicans by proposing a religious test. "Donald J. Trump is calling for a total and complete shutdown of Muslims entering the United States until our country's representatives can figure out what the hell is going on," he read aloud from a written statement. A day later, he elaborated, saying that customs agents would be directed to ask incoming travelers if they are Muslim, and that those who said yes would be turned away.

In May, with the Republican nomination his, Mr. Trump retreated slightly, now calling the ban merely an idea, not a proposal. "It's a temporary ban, it hasn't been called for yet," he said, adding, "This is just a suggestion until we find out what's going on."

On June 13, Mr. Trump offered a slightly new formulation: The ban would be geographical, not religious, applying to "areas of the world where there is a proven history of terrorism against the United States, Europe or our allies." But not just any kind of terrorism, he clarified on Twitter two hours later: The ban was only for nations "tied to Islamic terror." Then, in Scotland last weekend, Mr. Trump said he would allow Muslims from allies like the United Kingdom to enter the United States.

ABORTION

Mr. Trump, who supported abortion rights until 2011, has struggled to articulate his evolution to the anti-abortion camp and has shown a lack of fluency on the details. Pressed by MSNBC's Chris Matthews in March, he said that abortion should be banned and then said that women violating the ban should face "some sort of punishment." He recanted within hours, saying that doctors who perform abortions should be held legally responsible; women, he said, were the victims.

On Monday, when the Supreme Court overturned a Texas law that would have restricted access to abortions, many Republicans said the ruling was further evidence that a Republican president was needed to restore the court's conservative majority. But Mr. Trump, perhaps out of caution, remained silent.

MINIMUM WAGE

At a Republican presidential debate in November, Mr. Trump said that "wages are too high," and that American workers will need to "work really hard" if they want their incomes to rise. "I hate to say it, but we have to leave it where it is," he said.

Interviewed on CNN in May, Mr. Trump said he was "open" to raising the minimum wage, though he remained concerned about the ability of American companies to compete globally. "I'm very different from most Republicans," he said, acknowledging that the federal minimum wage of $7.25 was too low. "You have to have something that you can live on."

GAY RIGHTS

Mr. Trump was long known for his warmth toward gays, including Elton John, whose civil union he publicly applauded. But since he became a candidate, his views have meandered. He has consistently opposed same-sex marriage, speaking out last year against the Supreme Court decision that legalized it, and pledging to work to overturn that ruling.

In April, he thrilled some gay rights supporters when he weighed in on a transgender bathroom bill in North Carolina, saying that people should be allowed to use whatever restroom they felt comfortable in. But hours later, he said that states should make their own decisions.

Then, after the June 12 massacre at a gay nightclub in Orlando, Fla., Mr. Trump railed against the gunman for trying to hinder people's ability to "love who they want and express their identity" — language lifted right out of the gay marriage movement.

TORTURE

Mr. Trump rose to prominence by describing the United States' response to terrorism as flaccid. During a debate in February, he inched toward endorsing torture as a way to counteract the Islamic State's barbarism. "Not since medieval times have people seen what's going on," Mr. Trump said of hostages decapitated by the Islamic State. "I would bring back waterboarding, and I'd bring back a hell of a lot worse than waterboarding."

Later, he declared that "torture works," and called for killing the families of terrorists, a violation of international law. In March, he released a statement acknowledging the limitations imposed by laws and treaties and saying that he would not "order our military or other officials to violate those laws."

But just a day later, he told a crowd that he would seek to change the laws barring torture. "We're like a bunch of babies — but we're going to stay within the laws," he said. "But you know what we're going to do? We're going to have those laws broadened. Because we're playing with two sets of rules — their rules and our rules."

Donald Trump Keeps Distance in G.O.P. Platform Fight on Gay Rights

BY JEREMY W. PETERS | JULY 10, 2016

CLEVELAND — Same-sex marriage and transgender rights are emerging as points of serious strain between social conservatives and moderates who are trying to shape the Republican platform, reviving a festering cultural dispute as thousands of party activists and delegates prepare for their convention.

Caught in the middle is Donald J. Trump, who claims "tremendous support, tremendous friendship" from gays, lesbians, bisexuals and transgender people, and has gone further than most party figures to embrace them. Gays, in fact, are one of the few minority groups Mr. Trump has not singled out for criticism. But as the presumptive Republican nominee, he is also trying to assuage doubts about the convictions of his conservatism.

The uncomfortable dynamic Mr. Trump has created for himself is perhaps best illustrated by his own calendar.

He huddled last month at a Manhattan hotel with hundreds of religious conservatives, many of them — like James C. Dobson, the founder of Focus on the Family, and Tony Perkins, the president of the Family Research Council — outspoken opponents of new legal protections for gay and transgender people.

A few days later, he took what an aide described as a friendly and supportive call from Caitlyn Jenner, the former Olympic decathlete who came out as transgender last year.

One of the most contentious issues confronting delegates when they meet on Monday to debate the platform will be whether to adopt a provision defending state laws that try to prevent transgender people from using the public restroom of their choice. At times Mr. Trump has criticized those laws. And he has said Ms. Jenner can use whatever bathroom she prefers at his properties.

TY WRIGHT FOR THE NEW YORK TIMES

Donald Trump campaigning in Cincinnati. He has said he will not intervene in the writing of the Republican platform.

But he has also promised not to interfere with the platform, which serves as the party's official declaration of principles.

Even as Mr. Trump keeps his distance from the debate, other Republicans who share his more accepting view of gay and transgender issues are working aggressively to tone down some of the platform's language.

The existing platform, adopted in 2012, is replete with disapproval of homosexuality. It calls court decisions favoring same-sex marriage "an assault on the foundations of our society" and accuses the Obama administration of trying to impose "the homosexual rights agenda" on foreign countries.

Paul E. Singer, a billionaire Republican who has financed gay rights battles across the country, is now funding an effort to write into the platform language more inclusive of gays, lesbians and transgender people.

The goal of his group, the American Unity Fund, is not to get the party to endorse same-sex marriage but to add a more open-ended statement that commits the party "to respect for all families," though there is still fierce resistance from the right.

"We don't have to say we're tolerant because we are tolerant of other views," said James Bopp Jr., a member of the platform committee from Indiana who has long supported efforts to make the platform more strongly in favor of traditional marriage. Such language promoting tolerance, he added, would be "redundant and superfluous."

Advisers for the American Unity Fund, who say they know they are fighting a steep uphill battle, argue that the Republican Party can no longer afford to alienate people on gay rights issues.

"We've got to make room for people with diverse views on civil marriage," said Tyler Deaton, the group's senior adviser. "This platform doesn't even make room for people who support civil unions or domestic partnerships or people who support basic legal equality."

Both parties adopt new platforms at their conventions every four years. A draft of the 2016 version has been put together over the last several weeks by the Republican National Committee, with help from conservative activists. Members of the platform committee received the draft on Sunday evening and will add or change certain provisions over the next two days.

The draft circulating Sunday night condemned the Obama administration's effort to deny funding to states that prohibit transgender people from using the bathroom that aligns with their gender identity, accusing the administration of trying to impose a cultural revolution. "They are determined to reshape our schools — and our entire society — to fit the mold of an ideology alien to America's history," the draft reads. Another section criticizes those who boycott businesses that deny services to same-sex couples.

Though he will almost certainly not mention it when he accepts the nomination next week, Mr. Trump's actions and words on gay rights have been more supportive than those of any Republican presidential nominee, even if they fall short of the full social and legal acceptance that his expected opponent, Hillary Clinton, has promoted.

He has boasted of his friendships with many gay people, saying "I have so many fabulous friends who happen to be gay."

He has supported AIDS charities for years, and welcomed gay couples at his Palm Beach club when doing so was considered remarkable. And he has recently started insisting that he would be a better friend to the gay community than Mrs. Clinton, even though he opposes legal rights like marriage.

But as he tries to convince social conservatives that he is not acting as a moderate, Mr. Trump has been largely hands-off with the platform.

"His guys have not shown up and said, 'Change this, change that,' " David Barton, a platform committee member from Texas, said.

The Republican platform committee has long been dominated by some of the party's most stalwart activists. And some of them have hardly been shy about their views.

There is Cynthia Dunbar of Virginia, who has compared the gay rights movement to Nazism. Hardy Billington, a committee member from Missouri, placed an ad in a local paper asserting that homosexuality kills people at two to three times the rate of smoking. And Mary Frances Forrester of North Carolina has claimed that the "homosexual agenda is trying to change the course of Western civilization." Mr. Bopp of Indiana recently wrote to delegates to say that the Republican Party has always opposed threats to traditional marriage "beginning with our opposition to the 'twin relics of barbarism' of slavery and polygamy in our 1856 platform."

As dominant as those conservative voices have been, delegates who want to see a more inclusive platform are gaining seats on the committee.

Many of them believe the Republican Party needs to have a serious debate this year about whittling down a platform that has grown long and become riddled with special-interest additions.

Boyd Matheson, a first-time platform committee member from

Utah, noted that at 33,000 words, the 2012 platform was "six or seven times longer than the Constitution." Recent platforms have become, he said, "these laundry lists and litmus tests of 'thou shalts' and 'thou shalt nots.' "

The party's first platform in 1856 was fewer than 1,000 words.

As an alternative this year, Mr. Matheson proposed a 1,177-word document that he said adheres to the founding principles of the party, like equal rights and economic opportunity. It contains no mention of same-sex marriage or transgender issues. "That does not elevate the discussion we need," Mr. Matheson said.

It is not the discussion Mr. Trump is eager to have, either. Asked in a recent interview about the platform, he declined to comment, saying only that he was "looking at it."

But as a reminder of how unorthodox a Republican Mr. Trump is — and of how contrary many of his views on issues like trade, foreign policy, eminent domain and gay rights are to the party's doctrine — there is no more vivid example than the platform.

"The bigger problem for Trump and the Republican National Committee," said Lanhee J. Chen, who led Mitt Romney's platform efforts in 2012, "is the fact that there are these major disagreements between where Trump is on some of these issues and where the activist base of the party is."

Differences between a candidate's views and what is written in the platform are nothing new, of course. Bob Dole admitted he had not read the entire document when he was the Republican nominee in 1996. And he publicly repudiated parts of it that called for a constitutional amendment to deny automatic citizenship for children born to illegal immigrants.

It is not clear Mr. Trump would ever go that far, given how little attention he has paid to the party's traditions and sacraments.

"I don't know if Trump really cares," Mr. Chen added.

For Whites Sensing Decline, Donald Trump Unleashes Words of Resistance

BY NICHOLAS CONFESSORE | JULY 13, 2016

THE CHANT ERUPTS in a college auditorium in Washington, as admirers of a conservative internet personality shout down a black protester. It echoes around the gym of a central Iowa high school, as white students taunt the Hispanic fans and players of a rival team. It is hollered by a lone motorcyclist, as he tears out of a Kansas gas station after an argument with a Hispanic man and his Muslim friend.

Trump

Trump

Trump

In countless collisions of color and creed, Donald J. Trump's name evokes an easily understood message of racial hostility. Defying modern conventions of political civility and language, Mr. Trump has breached the boundaries that have long constrained Americans' public discussion of race.

Mr. Trump has attacked Mexicans as criminals. He has called for a ban on Muslim immigrants. He has wondered aloud why the United States is not "letting people in from Europe."

His rallies vibrate with grievances that might otherwise be expressed in private: about "political correctness," about the ranch house down the street overcrowded with day laborers, and about who is really to blame for the death of a black teenager in Ferguson, Mo. In a country where the wealthiest and most influential citizens are still mostly white, Mr. Trump is voicing the bewilderment and anger of whites who do not feel at all powerful or privileged.

But in doing so, Mr. Trump has also opened the door to assertions of white identity and resentment in a way not seen so broadly in American culture in over half a century, according to those who track patterns of racial tension and antagonism in American life.

Dozens of interviews — with ardent Trump supporters and curious students, avowed white nationalists, and scholars who study the interplay of race and rhetoric — suggest that the passions aroused and channeled by Mr. Trump take many forms, from earnest if muddled rebellion to deeper and more elaborate bigotry.

On campuses clenched by unforgiving debates over language and inclusion, some students embrace Mr. Trump as a way of rebelling against the intricate rules surrounding privilege and microaggression, and provoking the keepers of those rules.

Among older whites unsettled by new Spanish-speaking neighbors, or suspicious of the faith claimed by their country's most bitter enemies, his name is a call to arms.

On the internet, Mr. Trump is invoked by anonymous followers brandishing stark expressions of hate and anti-Semitism, surprisingly amplified this month when Mr. Trump tweeted a graphic depicting Hillary Clinton's face with piles of cash and a six-pointed star that many viewed as a Star of David.

"I think what we really find troubling is the mainstreaming of these really offensive ideas," said Jonathan Greenblatt, the national director of the Anti-Defamation League, which tracks hate groups. "It's allowed some of the worst ideas into the public conversation in ways we haven't seen anything like in recent memory."

Mr. Trump declined to be interviewed for this article, and his spokesman declined to comment.

Outside a former aircraft factory in Bethpage, N.Y., not far from a strip of halal butchers and Indian restaurants now known as Little India, a Long Island housewife who gave her name as Kathy Reb finished a cigarette on a spring evening. Nervously, she explained how she had watched the complexion of her suburb outside New York City change. "Everyone's sticking together in their groups," she said, "so white people have to, too."

The resentment among whites feels both old and distinctly of this moment. It is shaped by the reality of demographic change, by a decade and a half of war in the Middle East, and by unease with the newly confident and confrontational activism of young blacks furious over police violence. It is mingled with patriotism, pride, fear and a sense that an America without them at its center is not really America anymore.

In the months since Mr. Trump began his campaign, the percentage of Americans who say race relations are worsening has increased, reaching nearly half in an April poll by CBS News. The sharpest rise was among Republicans: Sixty percent said race relations were getting worse.

And Mr. Trump's rise is shifting the country's racial discourse just as the millennial generation comes fully of age, more and more distant from the horrors of the Holocaust, or the government-sanctioned racism of Jim Crow.

Some are elated by the turn. In making the explicit assertion of white identity and grievance more widespread, Mr. Trump has galvanized the otherwise marginal world of avowed white nationalists and self-described "race realists." They hail him as a fellow traveler who has driven millions of white Americans toward an intuitive embrace of their ideals: that race should matter as much to white people as it does to everyone else. He has freed Americans, those activists say, to say what they really believe.

"The discussion that white Americans never want to have is this question of identity — who are we?" said Richard Spencer, 38, a writer and an activist whose Montana-based nonprofit is dedicated to "the heritage, identity and future of people of European descent" in the United States. "He is bringing identity politics for white people into the public sphere in a way no one has."

IMMIGRATION FEARS

Another Republican once sounded alarms about globalization, unchecked immigration and the looming obsolescence of European-

STEPHEN CROWLEY/THE NEW YORK TIMES

Patrick J. Buchanan in 1995.

American culture. But in two bids for the Republican nomination, that candidate, Patrick J. Buchanan, won a total of four states. Mr. Trump won 37.

Mr. Buchanan's 1992 and 1996 campaigns were dismissed as a political and intellectual dead end for Republicans.

"I said, 'Look, we're the white party,' " Mr. Buchanan said in an interview from his Virginia home, recalling his attacks on multiculturalism and non-European immigration. " 'If this continues, we're going the way of the Whigs.' Everyone said, 'That's a terrible thing to say.' "

Mr. Buchanan was campaigning against a backdrop of overwhelming white political and cultural dominance in America. But in the years that followed, the number of immigrants living in the United States illegally would double and then triple, before leveling off under the Obama administration around 11 million. Deindustrialization, driven in part by global trade, would devastate the economic fortunes of white men accustomed to making a decent living without a college degree.

Demographers began to speak of a not-too-distant future when non-Hispanic whites would be a minority of the American population. In states like Texas and California, and in hundreds of cities and counties around the country, that future has arrived. "It is the changes that are taking place that have created the national constituency for Donald Trump," Mr. Buchanan said.

For many Americans, President Obama's election, made possible in part by the rising strength of nonwhite voters, signaled a transcendent moment in the country's knotty racial history. But for some whites, the election of the country's first black president was also a powerful symbol of their declining pre-eminence in American society.

Work by Michael I. Norton, a professor at Harvard Business School, suggests that whites have come to see anti-white bias as more prevalent than anti-black bias, and that they think further black progress is coming at their expense. On talk radio and Fox News, complaints about bigotry are routinely dismissed as a mere hustle — blacks "playing the race card" or being racist themselves. And during Mr. Obama's presidency, whites have increasingly seen his policies as freighted with preference toward blacks, according to data collected by Michael Tesler, a political scientist at the University of California, Irvine.

Mr. Tesler used polling questions about the causes and depth of racial inequality — such as whether blacks suffer greater poverty because of discrimination or lack of effort — to classify people as either "racial conservatives" or "racial liberals." During Mr. Obama's two terms, Mr. Tesler found, racial liberals accelerated their migration to the Democratic Party. As the 2016 campaign began, the Republican Party was not just the party of most white voters. It was also, to use Mr. Tesler's phrase, the party of racial conservatism.

Few politicians were better prepared than Mr. Trump to harness these shifts. While open racism against blacks remains among the most powerful taboos in American politics, Americans feel more free expressing worries about illegal immigrants and dislike of Islam, survey research shows. In Mr. Trump's hands, the two ideas merged: During Mr. Obama's presidency, he has become America's most prominent "birther," loudly questioning Mr. Obama's American citizenship and suggesting he could be Muslim.

When Mr. Obama ran for re-election, few Americans said they disapproved of him because of his race. But they were comfortable citing his supposed religion. In 2012, according to surveys conducted for the Cooperative Congressional Election Study, a majority of Mitt Romney's voters said Mr. Obama's religion made them less likely to vote for him. Almost all of these voters believed he was not Christian, an opinion that closely correlated with conservative racial attitudes found in Mr. Tesler's research.

Mr. Trump "is speaking an anti-other message — that Obama's foreign, which is mixed in with being black, and perceptions that he is Muslim," Mr. Tesler said. "It is a catchall for expressing ethnocentric opposition to Obama, without saying you're against him because he's black."

A VAGUE REFRAIN: 'I DISAVOW'

In June 2015, two weeks after Mr. Trump entered the presidential race, he received an endorsement that would end most campaigns: The Daily Stormer embraced his candidacy.

Founded in 2013 by a neo-Nazi named Andrew Anglin, The Daily Stormer is among the most prominent online gathering places for white nationalists and anti-Semites, with sections devoted to "The Jewish Problem" and "Race War." Mr. Anglin, 31, explained that although he had some disagreements with him, Mr. Trump was the only candidate willing to speak the truth about Mexicans.

"Trump is willing to say what most Americans think: It's time to deport these people," Mr. Anglin wrote. "He is also willing to call them out as criminal rapists, murderers and drug dealers."

They had long been absent from mainstream politics, taking refuge at obscure conferences and in largely anonymous havens online. Most believed that the Republican Party had been subverted and captured by liberal racial dictums.

Many in this new generation of nationalists shun the trappings of old-fashioned white supremacy, appropriating the language of multiculturalism to recast themselves as white analogues to La Raza and other civil rights organizations. They call themselves "race realists" or "identitarians" — conservatives for whom racial heritage is more important than ideology.

But across this spectrum, in Mr. Trump's descriptions of immigrants as vectors of disease, violent crime and social decay, they heard their own dialect.

Mr. Spencer, a popular figure in the white nationalist world, said he did not believe that Mr. Trump subscribed to his entire worldview.

TIM GOESSMAN FOR THE NEW YORK TIMES

Richard Spencer, a white nationalist in Montana, said Mr. Trump was "bringing identity politics for white people into the public sphere in a way no one has."

But he was struck that Mr. Trump seemed to understand and echo many of his group's ideas intuitively, and take them to a broader audience.

"I don't think he has thought through this issue in a way that I and a number of people have," Mr. Spencer said. "I think he is reacting to the feeling that he has lost his country."

This year, for the first time in decades, overt white nationalism re-entered national politics. In Iowa, a new "super PAC" paid for pro-Trump robocalls featuring Jared Taylor, a self-described race realist, and William Johnson, a white nationalist and the chairman of the American Freedom Party. ("We don't need Muslims," Mr. Taylor urged recipients of the calls. "We need smart, well-educated white people who will assimilate to our culture. Vote Trump.") David Duke, the Louisiana lawmaker turned anti-Semitic radio host, encouraged listeners to vote for Mr. Trump.

Modern political convention dictates that candidates receiving such embraces instantly and publicly spurn them. In 2008, when it was revealed that a minister who endorsed the Republican nominee, Senator John McCain, had made anti-Semitic and anti-Muslim remarks, Mr. McCain forcefully repudiated them.

Mr. Trump did something different.

Asked about the robocall, Mr. Trump seemed to sympathize with its message while affecting a vague half-distance. "Nothing in this country shocks me; I would disavow it, but nothing in this country shocks me," Mr. Trump told a CNN anchor. "People are angry."

Pressed, Mr. Trump grew irritable, saying: "How many times you want me to say it? I said, 'I disavow.' "

Asked six weeks later about Mr. Duke's support, he said he had been unaware of it: "David Duke endorsed me? O.K. All right. I disavow, O.K.?" Later, on Twitter, he repeated the phrase: "I disavow."

Mr. Trump has often used those words when confronted by reporters. The phrase is comfortingly nonspecific, a disavowal of everything and nothing. And whatever Mr. Trump's intentions, it has been powerfully reassuring to people on the far right.

"There's no direct object there," Mr. Spencer said. "It's kind of interesting, isn't it?"

Mr. Trump's new supporters took his approach as a signal of support. In an interview on a "pro-white" radio show called "The Political Cesspool," Mr. Johnson, of the American Freedom Party, praised Mr. Trump's handling of the controversy.

"He disavowed us," Mr. Johnson acknowledged, "but he explained why there is so much anger in America that I couldn't have asked for a better approach from him."

Mr. Taylor, who has written that blacks "left entirely to their own devices" are incapable of civilization, and whose magazine, American Renaissance, once published an essay arguing that blacks were genetically more prone to crime, wrote on his blog that Mr. Trump had handled the attacks on him "in the nicest way."

Like others in his world, Mr. Taylor does not know if Mr. Trump agrees with him on everything. In an interview, he suggested that it

JUSTIN T. GELLERSON FOR THE NEW YORK TIMES

Jared Taylor, a self-described race realist, made robocalls urging Iowa voters to support Mr. Trump.

did not really matter, and that Mr. Trump was expressing the discomfort many white people felt about other races.

"Ordinary white people don't want the neighborhood to turn Mexican," Mr. Taylor said, adding, "They just realize that large numbers of Mexicans will change the neighborhood in ways they don't like."

At a Trump rally last month in Richmond, Va., as at most Trump rallies, the audience was mostly white men. They strolled by police barricades in work boots or pressed khakis, grinning at a ragtag assortment of protesters nearby. In interviews, they complained about the Mexican flags brandished outside Trump events and wondered why the government was paying to fix up Section 8 houses for people with late-model iPhones. They recounted Hispanic co-workers mocking them.

"They'll tell you straight to your face, 'This is our country now — no more gringos!' " said Nick Conrad, a sheet metal worker who wore a "Hillary Clinton for Prison" T-shirt and wraparound sunglasses. "They're not in it for our culture. They're not here to assimilate."

Mr. Conrad shrugged.

"He says what everyone thinks," Mr. Conrad said of Mr. Trump. "He says what we're all thinking. He's bringing people together. We say, 'Hey, that's right; we can say this.' "

RETWEETS AND REPERCUSSIONS

Mr. Trump dismisses those who accuse him of embracing or enabling racism. "I'm the least racist person," he declared in December in an interview with CNN.

But on the flatlands of social media, the border between Mr. Trump and white supremacists easily blurs. He has retweeted supportive messages from racist or nationalist Twitter accounts to his nine million followers. Last fall, he retweeted a graphic with fictitious crime statistics claiming that 81 percent of white homicide victims in 2015 were killed by blacks. (No such statistic was available for 2015 at the time; the actual figure for 2014 was 15 percent, according to the F.B.I.)

In January and February he retweeted messages from a user with the handle @WhiteGenocideTM, whose profile picture is of George Lincoln Rockwell, the founder of the American Nazi Party. A couple of days later, in quick succession, he retweeted two more accounts featuring white nationalist or Nazi themes. Mr. Trump deleted one of the retweets, but white supremacists saw more than a twitch of the thumb. “Our Glorious Leader and ULTIMATE SAVIOR has gone full wink-wink-wink to his most aggressive supporters,” Mr. Anglin wrote on The Daily Stormer.

In fact, Mr. Trump’s Twitter presence is tightly interwoven with hordes of mostly anonymous accounts trafficking in racist and anti-Semitic attacks. When Little Bird, a social media data mining company, analyzed a week of Mr. Trump’s Twitter activity, it found that almost 30 percent of the accounts Mr. Trump retweeted in turn followed one or more of 50 popular self-identified white nationalist accounts.

At times, a circular current seems to flow between white nationalists and Mr. Trump on Twitter. Criticized for his recent message about Mrs. Clinton, Mr. Trump insisted that no allusion to Jews was intended and denounced reporters for drawing the connection. Mr. Trump’s social media director said in a statement that he had “lifted” the image from an anti-Clinton Twitter feed where “countless images appear.” Among them, it turned out, was a series of photos of Mrs. Clinton’s head arranged in the shape of a swastika.

The original image was later traced by Mic, an online magazine aimed at younger readers, to the politics section of 8chan, a message board riddled with anti-Semitic memes and racist images. There and on other message boards, such as 4chan and Reddit, Mr. Trump’s attacks on political correctness and illegal immigration resonate with a broader audience. Some claim membership in the “alt-right,” a loose and contested term that can encompass white nationalists, anti-immigration conservatives and anonymous trolls whose taunts are laced with GIFs and obscure internet slang.

After Mr. Trump attacked a profile of his wife, Melania, in GQ, the article's author, the journalist Julia Ioffe, who is Jewish, was inundated with anti-Semitic abuse on social media, including a cartoon depicting Ms. Ioffe in a concentration camp.

Asked whether he condemned the attacks, Mr. Trump told an interviewer: "I don't have a message to the fans. A woman wrote an article that's inaccurate."

RESONATING ON CAMPUSES

Mr. Trump's influence is playing out perhaps most vividly on college campuses, an otherwise deeply liberal redoubt where young people grapple openly and frenetically with their own race and identity.

For a generation weaned on a diet of civic multiculturalism, supporting Mr. Trump breaks the ultimate taboo. Students writing Mr. Trump's name and slogans in chalk have been accused of hate crimes and spurred calls for censorship. And on campuses frozen by unyielding political correctness and expanding definitions of impermissible speech, some welcome the provocation that Mr. Trump provides.

Three days after a gunman claiming allegiance to the Islamic State killed 49 people in a gay club in Orlando, Fla., a crowd of college students gathered two blocks from the site of the massacre. They wore Trump hats or T-shirts and chanted, "Build that wall." They cracked jokes about trigger warnings or whether the sidewalk counted as a safe space.

A few minutes later, a black S.U.V. pulled up, delivering Milo Yiannopoulos, a 30-something gay conservative raised in London and now a minor celebrity among the alt-right.

Since 2014, Mr. Yiannopoulos has toured college campuses in the United States and England, staging a performance that is equal parts spectacle and stump speech. Mr. Yiannopoulos dismisses statistics on campus rape as an official fiction and favors the slogan "Feminism is a cancer."

His barbs are directed chiefly at liberals, feminists and Black Lives Matter activists, all of whom routinely show up to protest or disrupt his speeches. His followers film these confrontations and share them enthusiastically on YouTube and Facebook. In one video, Mr. Yiannopoulos arrives at a speech on a sedan chair carried by several young men wearing Trump hats.

"I knew I could have fun on campuses because they are so uptight and they are so ruled by the people I don't like," said Mr. Yiannopoulos, who considers himself a "free-speech fundamentalist." He added, "Less cynically, they're an important battleground."

Shortly after the shooting, Mr. Yiannopoulos announced plans to speak at the University of Central Florida in Orlando. The university canceled his appearance, first citing a shortage of security personnel and then claiming that no suitable space was available on the 1,415-acre campus. Instead, Mr. Yiannopoulos spoke near the nightclub.

He stood just feet from the network television encampments, though none had sent cameras or reporters to cover him. Wearing a dark pinstriped suit under the unrelenting Florida sun, he warned of a gathering menace from Muslim immigrants, sprinkling his speech with anecdotes about sexual assaults in Germany and gender-segregated swimming pools.

In Mr. Yiannopoulos's telling, liberals were dupes and hypocrites, so blinded by glib multiculturalism that they could not even admit how dangerous Islam was to gay people, like the victims of the Orlando massacre. To cheers and whoops, he praised Mr. Trump's plan to bar Muslims from entering the country.

Afterward, fans lined up to get his autograph. Most seemed to be Trump supporters, but not all were conservative. Several described themselves as socially liberal or libertarian. A few said they just wanted to hear what Mr. Yiannopoulos had to say.

"The setup of U.C.F. has very few places where people are allowed to speak," said Allen Greathouse, a slender 20-year-old from Melbourne, Fla. "You can only speak in the free-speech zones."

Another student, Simon Dickerman, said he was voting for Mr. Trump. He volunteered that he frequently visited 4chan, an online message board where users compete with one another to post ever more provocative content, from Nazi shorthand to racist cartoons.

Mr. Dickerman said he understood why such images bothered some older people, though they carried little such charge to him and his friends.

"Of course they don't actually want Jews to die," Mr. Dickerman said. "They want to shock." His peers, he added, "are kids who don't really know about the Holocaust."

"And they don't care about history," he said. "And some of them think it's funny."

MAGGIE HABERMAN AND KITTY BENNETT CONTRIBUTED REPORTING.

U.S. Says Russia Directed Hacks to Influence Elections

BY DAVID E. SANGER AND CHARLIE SAVAGE | OCT. 7, 2016

WASHINGTON — The Obama administration on Friday formally accused the Russian government of stealing and disclosing emails from the Democratic National Committee and a range of other institutions and prominent individuals, immediately raising the issue of whether President Obama would seek sanctions or other retaliation.

In a statement from the director of national intelligence, James R. Clapper Jr., and the Department of Homeland Security, the government said the leaked emails that have appeared on a variety of websites "are intended to interfere with the U.S. election process."

The emails were posted on the well-known WikiLeaks site and two newer sites, DCLeaks.com and Guccifer 2.0, identified as being associated with Russian intelligence.

"We believe, based on the scope and sensitivity of these efforts, that only Russia's senior-most officials could have authorized these activities," the statement said.

It did not name President Vladimir V. Putin of Russia, but that appeared to be the intention.

The statement from Mr. Clapper and the Department of Homeland Security, which is primarily responsible for defending the country against sophisticated cyberattacks, said the intelligence agencies were less certain who was responsible for "scanning and probing" online election rolls in states around the country. It said that those "in most cases originated from servers operated by a Russian company," but stopped short of alleging the Russian government was responsible for those probes.

The announcement came only hours after Secretary of State John Kerry called for the Russian and Syrian governments to face a formal war-crimes investigation over attacks on civilians in Aleppo and other parts of Syria. Taken together, the developments mark a sharp escalation of Washington's many confrontations with Moscow this year.

For weeks, aides to Mr. Obama have been debating whether to openly attribute the cyberattacks to Russia, and as recently as Wednesday the director of the National Security Agency, Adm. Michael Rogers, refused to publicly accuse Moscow.

But with little more than a month to go before the presidential election, one senior administration official said that Mr. Obama was "under pressure to act now," in part because a declaration closer to Election Day would appear to be political. Two days ahead of the second presidential debate, the announcement also puts the Republican nominee, Donald J. Trump, more on the defensive over his assertion last month that Mr. Putin is a better leader than Mr. Obama.

In the first debate, former Secretary of State Hillary Clinton, Mr. Trump's Democratic rival, blamed Russia for the cyberattacks on the Democratic National Committee, but Mr. Trump said there was no evidence that Russia was responsible; he suggested it could have been the Chinese or "somebody sitting on their bed that weighs 400 pounds."

Soon after the administration accused the Russians of hacking into the committee, WikiLeaks published hacked emails from John D. Podesta, the Clinton campaign chairman.

In a Twitter message Friday evening, Mr. Podesta said that "I'm not happy about being hacked by the Russians in their attempt to throw the election to Donald Trump."

WikiLeaks has released troves of hacked Democratic emails, but has not revealed their source.

A major question is how Mr. Obama might respond without setting off an escalating cyberspace conflict with Russia between now and Nov. 8. One possibility is that the announcement itself — an effort to "name and shame" — will deter further action.

But Mr. Obama's aides have assembled a range of possible responses, from using economic sanctions to covert action against Russian targets, potentially including the computers used in the hack.

The official accusation against Russia comes after anonymous American intelligence officials told The New York Times in July that they had "high confidence" that the Russian government was behind the hack of the D.N.C., which led to the resignation of Representative Debbie Wasserman Schultz, the Florida Democrat, as committee chairwoman, amid evidence that the committee was favoring Mrs. Clinton over her competitor for the party nomination, Senator Bernie Sanders of Vermont.

The months of subsequent silence frustrated some in Congress, and several weeks ago the top Democrats on the House and Senate intelligence committees, Adam Schiff and Dianne Feinstein, both of California, said Russia and its leaders were responsible, citing classified briefings.

Mr. Schiff, who had urged the Obama administration to name Russia and better prepare American voters for the possibility of interference between now and the election, on Friday praised the decision "to call out Russia on its malevolent interference in our political affairs."

"I hope this will establish a deterrent to further meddling," he said. "I don't think the Russians have decided yet how much they plan to continue their interference, so I think this attribution is very timely. We're also encouraging the administration to work with our European partners, who have been the subject of even worse meddling, to coordinate a response to this."

Mr. Schiff said he was afraid Russian hackers might attempt to delete or manipulate voter rolls, causing long lines at the polls and delays in counting votes because people would be forced to cast provisional ballots. (Voting machines themselves are not linked to the internet, so it is effectively impossible to hack them in a systematic way and change the outcome, specialists say.)

But as "profound" as that concern is, Mr. Schiff said, he and others see as "the most grave risk" something else: Russia could take emails it has already stolen, manipulate them to create a false impression that a candidate has done something outrageous or illegal, and cause them to be published online shortly before the election.

That, he said, "could have an election-altering effect."

Federal officials are trying to help states plug holes in their internet defenses for election management systems. One thing they will not do before the election is pronounce such systems "critical infrastructure," as the secretary of Homeland Security, Jeh Johnson, proposed in August.

Mr. Johnson's notion provoked a backlash from conservatives. Republicans like Brian P. Kemp, the secretary of state in Georgia, and Jon A. Husted, his counterpart in Ohio, accused the Obama administration of overreaching, saying it was trying to carry out a federal takeover.

Administration officials said that the idea of declaring elections systems critical infrastructure is dead for now, lest it discourage states from working with the federal government.

"Our focus right now, in the remaining days before Nov. 8, is to encourage states to come forward and request our assistance," Mr. Johnson said in a recent interview.

The department has offered states two kinds of help, both for free: a remote cyber "hygiene" scan of their servers by department officials who look for known vulnerabilities and can recommend patches, and a more intensive on-site analysis by a team of computer security specialists.

The department's emphasis on voluntary measures has met with mixed success: So far, 28 states have accepted that offer, the department said, but it declined to name them. Officials with election agencies in the large swing states of Ohio, North Carolina and Pennsylvania said they were participating. (Pennsylvania is particularly important because its electronic voting machines lack a paper audit trail for recounts.)

Florida, another large swing state, is not participating in this program, but officials in the office of its secretary of state said they had already been working with federal partners.

Still, while the number of participants has been slowly creeping up, the window is closing. A Homeland Security official said it takes about a week to complete the necessary paperwork to permit the department to begin the work, and that the more intensive on-site effort takes about two weeks.

That suggests that soon after the middle of October, it will be too late to provide any help to late takers.

The fact that 22 states are not as yet participating does not necessarily mean all of them are vulnerable in ways that participants are not. Kay Stimson, a spokeswoman for the National Association of Secretaries of State, noted that some states had already been taking cybersecurity measures that are likely equivalent to what the department is offering.

Donald Trump's Apology That Wasn't

BY MAGGIE HABERMAN | OCT. 8, 2016

FOR HOURS on Friday night, the political world waited for the rarest of expressions from Donald J. Trump — a heartfelt apology.

What viewers got was anything but.

During a 90-second videotaped appearance, Mr. Trump, the Republican presidential nominee, offered a strikingly brief articulation of regret for a decade-old audiotape in which he boasted about grabbing women's genitals and said he could have his way with women because of his fame.

But his real message, which appeared early Saturday, was one of defiance. He described the controversy that upended the Republican Party for most of Friday as a mere "distraction," and said that his vulgar remarks captured on the tape were nothing compared with the way Bill and Hillary Clinton had mistreated women.

If anything, Mr. Trump's videotaped statement was a truncated version of a speech that he had given countless times. And it did not reflect the several hours of conference calls and strategy meetings among his top aides, who were at first stunned and then nearly paralyzed by the revelation of the tape, which they worried would be fatal to his White House hopes.

"That took 10 hours?" an incredulous Kevin Madden, a Republican strategist, asked on CNN immediately after the statement.

With his brow furrowed and his face a tight scowl, Mr. Trump sat hunched in a chair inside Trump Tower on Fifth Avenue, with the glittering nighttime New York City skyline behind him.

"I've never said I'm a perfect person, nor pretended to be someone that I'm not," said Mr. Trump, a 70-year-old real estate developer and former reality television star.

Then came the apologetic part.

"I've said and done things I regret, and the words released today on this more-than-a-decade-old video are one of them," Mr. Trump said of the hot-mike recording of him bragging to Billy Bush, then the host of NBC's "Access Hollywood," about his groping and uninvited kissing of women.

"Anyone who knows me knows these words don't reflect who I am," Mr. Trump continued.

"I said it, I was wrong, and I apologize," he said.

Oddly, Mr. Trump seemed to frame his comments not as sincere concern about those he may have hurt or offended, but as part of his own journey, describing his growth as a person and how humbling it has been for him to campaign across the nation and learn of other people's worries and travails.

"I've traveled the country talking about change for America, but my travels have also changed me," he said, describing meeting mothers who have lost children and people who have lost their jobs.

"I pledge to be a better man tomorrow and will never, ever let you down," Mr. Trump said.

Grudging though they seemed, Mr. Trump's comments were a marked departure from his lifelong resistance to any admission of fault. Mr. Trump values strength and power and disparages weakness. His usual response, when criticized or hurt, has been to counterpunch forcefully.

Before the release of the short statement, advisers to Mr. Trump had huddled with him at Trump Tower, along with his daughter Ivanka and son-in-law Jared Kushner, to discuss how to respond to the crisis. The advisers cautioned against holding a news conference, something that had been discussed, because it could become unwieldy and spin out of his control. They realized they needed to address the issue quickly, at a minimum to try to stop the defections of Republican officials who had begun to shun and loudly denounce him. But one adviser to Mr. Trump cautioned before the statement that if the candidate mentioned Mrs. Clinton, it would fail.

Mr. Trump did just that.

"Hillary Clinton and her kind have run our country into the ground," Mr. Trump said. "I've said some foolish things, but there's a big difference between the words and actions of other people. Bill Clinton has actually abused women, and Hillary has bullied, attacked, shamed and intimidated his victims."

Mr. Trump then turned the focus to his second debate against Mrs. Clinton, less than 48 hours away.

Ever the performer and intimidator, he added, with a hint of menace in his voice: "We will discuss this more in the coming days. See you at the debate on Sunday."

CHAPTER 3

The Transition

Donald Trump's campaign victory shocked much of the United States and the world. Political pundits and academics were alerted to the wide divisions in the United States across economic, cultural and political lines. Facebook data had been compromised in order to target political ads, leading to the spread of fake news and further dividing the American public. And in the wake of victory, Trump's preparations to take office confused and alarmed many. The new administration was characterized by hirings, conflict and firings well before the inauguration in January 2017.

Presidential Election Live: Donald Trump's Victory

BY MICHAEL D. SHEAR | NOV. 8, 2016

DONALD J. TRUMP'S victory in the presidential race on Tuesday night capped a remarkable election in which several Democratic Senate candidates fell short and Republicans retained their majority in the House of Representatives. Here are some key takeaways from a stunning result that upended conventional expectations and set the stage for a drastic reordering of politics in Washington:

• Mr. Trump took the stage at the Hilton just before 3 a.m. and told his supporters that Hillary Clinton called him to concede the election. Striking a gracious note, he wished her well and said, "We owe her a major debt of gratitude for her debt to our country."

• Reading from teleprompters and flanked by Gov. Mike Pence of Indiana and his son, Barron, Mr. Trump said he wanted to "reclaim our country's destiny" and be bold and daring. He also called for unity and said that he hoped Democrats and Republicans would work together.

• Democratic hopes that Hillary Clinton would easily defeat Mr. Trump crumbled as the evening wore on, as the Republican candidate's bombastic style appeared to win significant support among white, working-class and rural voters across the country.

• Mrs. Clinton's loss seemed to result, in part, from a worse-than-expected showing among African-Americans and young voters — two important parts of the coalition that lifted President Obama to victories in 2008 and 2012.

• Black voters made up 12 percent of the national electorate this year, nearly the same as in 2012. Mrs. Clinton won a broad majority of black voters — 88 percent, compared with 8 percent for Mr. Trump. But Mr. Obama received 93 percent of the African-American vote four years ago.

• Mrs. Clinton also did slightly worse than Mr. Obama among young voters. People under 30 made up 19 percent of this year's electorate, the same as in 2012. Mrs. Clinton got 54 percent of their support, compared with Mr. Obama's 60 percent. Mr. Trump had the backing of 37 percent of voters under 30, the same percentage that Mitt Romney won in 2012.

• Mr. Trump won in part on his strength with voters who were not strongly identified with either party. Independents made up 31 percent of 2016 voters, compared with 29 percent in 2012. Mrs. Clinton won 42 percent of independents, compared with Mr. Trump's 47 percent, while 6 percent voted for Gary Johnson and 3 percent supported Jill Stein.

• In the key battleground of Florida, Mr. Trump built his support largely on voters who expressed deep dismay with Washington. Nearly nine in 10 of his voters in Florida said they were dissatisfied or angry with the state of the federal government. Just as many disapproved of Mr. Obama's job performance, and three-quarters thought the president's health care law went too far.

• Nearly four in 10 Florida voters said they were most interested in electing a president who would bring serious change, and Mr. Trump won that group by a broad margin. Mrs. Clinton won voters looking for a compassionate, experienced or more judicious leader — but it was not enough to cancel out Mr. Trump's support among those hungry for change.

• Hispanic voters made up 11 percent of voters nationwide in 2016, just 1 point higher than in 2012. While Mrs. Clinton got 65 percent support among Hispanics, compared with 29 percent for Mr. Trump, her support from this group was six points lower than Mr. Obama's in 2012.

• While Mrs. Clinton did better than Mr. Trump among nonwhite voters in Florida, it was not enough to offset his success with white voters, who skew older in the state. He won those by nearly two to one, including those with a college degree. One-quarter of Florida's electorate was white and over 60. Mr. Trump pulled most of his support from the Gulf Coast and the central part of the state, a hub for wealthy retirees, offsetting Mrs. Clinton's gaping lead in the Miami and Orlando areas.

• Mr. Trump also did well in Ohio, where voters ages 18 to 29 were 11 points less likely to support the Democratic candidate this year than in 2012, with Mr. Johnson and Ms. Stein capturing 7 percent of their votes. Black voters in Ohio were six points less likely to support Mrs. Clinton than they were to support Mr. Obama four years ago.

• In North Carolina, 30 percent of voters were nonwhite, and Mrs. Clinton won this group by a 62-point margin (79 percent to 17 percent). Mr. Trump, countering with a strong showing among whites, won the state.

• The suburban share of the North Carolina vote increased to 38 percent, from 28 percent in 2012, while the share of the rural vote decreased by 10 points, to 24 percent. Mr. Trump won majorities in both groups.

AMY CHOZICK CONTRIBUTED REPORTING FROM CHAPPAQUA, N.Y.; SYDNEY EMBER FROM NEW YORK; NICHOLAS FANDOS FROM INDIANAPOLIS; THOMAS KAPLAN FROM RICHMOND, VA.; AND RACHEL SHOREY FROM WASHINGTON.

Donald Trump Is Elected President in Stunning Repudiation of the Establishment

BY MATT FLEGENHEIMER AND MICHAEL BARBARO | NOV. 9, 2016

DONALD JOHN TRUMP was elected the 45th president of the United States on Tuesday in a stunning culmination of an explosive, populist and polarizing campaign that took relentless aim at the institutions and long-held ideals of American democracy.

The surprise outcome, defying late polls that showed Hillary Clinton with a modest but persistent edge, threatened convulsions throughout the country and the world, where skeptics had watched with alarm as Mr. Trump's unvarnished overtures to disillusioned voters took hold.

The triumph for Mr. Trump, 70, a real estate developer-turned-reality television star with no government experience, was a powerful rejection of the establishment forces that had assembled against him, from the world of business to government, and the consensus they had forged on everything from trade to immigration.

The results amounted to a repudiation, not only of Mrs. Clinton, but of President Obama, whose legacy is suddenly imperiled. And it was a decisive demonstration of power by a largely overlooked coalition of mostly blue-collar white and working-class voters who felt that the promise of the United States had slipped their grasp amid decades of globalization and multiculturalism.

In Mr. Trump, a thrice-married Manhattanite who lives in a marble-wrapped three-story penthouse apartment on Fifth Avenue, they found an improbable champion.

"The forgotten men and women of our country will be forgotten no longer," Mr. Trump told supporters around 3 a.m. on Wednesday at a rally in New York City, just after Mrs. Clinton called to concede.

In a departure from a blistering campaign in which he repeatedly stoked division, Mr. Trump sought to do something he had conspicuously avoided as a candidate: Appeal for unity.

"Now it's time for America to bind the wounds of division," he said. "It is time for us to come together as one united people. It's time."

That, he added, "is so important to me."

He offered unusually warm words for Mrs. Clinton, who he has suggested should be in jail, saying she was owed "a major debt of gratitude for her service to our country."

Bolstered by Mr. Trump's strong showing, Republicans retained control of the Senate. Only one Republican-controlled seat, in Illinois, fell to Democrats early in the evening. And Senator Richard Burr of North Carolina, a Republican, easily won re-election in a race that had been among the country's most competitive. A handful of other Republican incumbents facing difficult races were running better than expected.

Mr. Trump's win — stretching across the battleground states of Florida, North Carolina, Ohio and Pennsylvania — seemed likely to set off financial jitters and immediate unease among international allies, many of which were startled when Mr. Trump in his campaign cast doubt on the necessity of America's military commitments abroad and its allegiance to international economic partnerships.

From the moment he entered the campaign, with a shocking set of claims that Mexican immigrants were rapists and criminals, Mr. Trump was widely underestimated as a candidate, first by his opponents for the Republican nomination and later by Mrs. Clinton, his Democratic rival. His rise was largely missed by polling organizations and data analysts. And an air of improbability trailed his campaign, to the detriment of those who dismissed his angry message, his improvisational style and his appeal to disillusioned voters.

He suggested remedies that raised questions of constitutionality, like a ban on Muslims entering the United States.

He threatened opponents, promising lawsuits against news organizations that covered him critically and women who accused him of sexual assault. At times, he simply lied.

But Mr. Trump's unfiltered rallies and unshakable self-regard attracted a zealous following, fusing unsubtle identity politics with an economic populism that often defied party doctrine.

His rallies — furious, entertaining, heavy on name-calling and nationalist overtones — became the nexus of a political movement, with daily promises of sweeping victory, in the election and otherwise, and an insistence that the country's political machinery was "rigged" against Mr. Trump and those who admired him.

He seemed to embody the success and grandeur that so many of his followers felt was missing from their own lives — and from the country itself. And he scoffed at the poll-driven word-parsing ways of modern politics, calling them a waste of time and money. Instead, he relied on his gut.

At his victory party at the New York Hilton Midtown, where a raucous crowd indulged in a cash bar and wore hats bearing his ubiquitous campaign slogan "Make America Great Again," voters expressed gratification that their voices had, at last, been heard.

"He was talking to people who weren't being spoken to," said Joseph Gravagna, 37, a marketing company owner from Rockland County, N.Y. "That's how I knew he was going to win."

For Mrs. Clinton, the defeat signaled an astonishing end to a political dynasty that has colored Democratic politics for a generation. Eight years after losing to President Obama in the Democratic primary — and 16 years after leaving the White House for the United States Senate, as President Bill Clinton exited office — she had seemed positioned to carry on two legacies: her husband's and the president's.

Her shocking loss was a devastating turn for the sprawling world of Clinton aides and strategists who believed they had built an electoral machine that would swamp Mr. Trump's ragtag band of loyal operatives and family members, many of whom had no experience running a national campaign.

On Tuesday night, stricken Clinton aides who believed that Mr. Trump had no mathematical path to victory, anxiously paced the Jacob K. Javits Convention Center as states in which they were confident of victory, like Florida and North Carolina, either fell to Mr. Trump or seemed in danger of tipping his way.

Mrs. Clinton watched the grim results roll in from a suite at the nearby Peninsula Hotel, surrounded by her family, friends and advisers who had the day before celebrated her candidacy with a champagne toast on her campaign plane.

But over and over, Mrs. Clinton's weaknesses as a candidate were exposed. She failed to excite voters hungry for change. She struggled to build trust with Americans who were baffled by her decision to use a private email server as secretary of state. And she strained to make a persuasive case for herself as a champion of the economically downtrodden after delivering perfunctory paid speeches that earned her millions of dollars.

The returns Tuesday also amounted to a historic rebuke of the Democratic Party from the white blue-collar voters who had formed the party base from the presidency of Franklin D. Roosevelt to Mr. Clinton's. Yet Mrs. Clinton and her advisers had taken for granted that states like Michigan and Wisconsin would stick with a Democratic nominee, and that she could repeat Mr. Obama's strategy of mobilizing the party's ascendant liberal coalition rather than pursuing a more moderate course like her husband did 24 years ago.

But not until these voters were offered a Republican who ran as an unapologetic populist, railing against foreign trade deals and illegal immigration, did they move so drastically away from their ancestral political home.

To the surprise of many on the left, white voters who had helped elect the nation's first black president, appeared more reluctant to line up behind a white woman.

From Pennsylvania to Wisconsin, industrial towns once full of union voters who for decades offered their votes to Democratic presidential candidates, even in the party's lean years, shifted to Mr. Trump's Republican Party. One county in the Mahoning Valley of Ohio, Trumbull, went to Mr. Trump by a six-point margin. Four years ago, Mr. Obama won there by 22 points.

Mrs. Clinton's loss was especially crushing to millions who had cheered her march toward history as, they hoped, the nation's first female president. For supporters, the election often felt like a referendum on gender progress: an opportunity to elevate a woman to the nation's top job and to repudiate a man whose remarkably boorish behavior toward women had assumed center stage during much of the campaign.

Mr. Trump boasted, in a 2005 video released last month, about using his public profile to commit sexual assault. He suggested that female political rivals lacked a presidential "look." He ranked women on a scale of one to 10, even holding forth on the desirability of his own daughter — the kind of throwback male behavior that many in the country assumed would disqualify a candidate for high office.

On Tuesday, the public's verdict was rendered.

Uncertainty abounds as Mr. Trump prepares to take office. His campaign featured a shape-shifting list of policy proposals, often seeming to change hour to hour. His staff was in constant turmoil, with Mr. Trump's children serving critical campaign roles and a rotating cast of advisers alternately seeking access to Mr. Trump's ear, losing it and, often, regaining it, depending on the day.

Even Mr. Trump's full embrace of the Republican Party came exceedingly late in life, leaving members of both parties unsure about what he truly believes. He has donated heavily to both parties and has long described his politics as the transactional reality of a businessman.

Mr. Trump's dozens of business entanglements — many of them in foreign countries — will follow him into the Oval Office, raising questions about potential conflicts of interest. His refusal to release his tax returns, and his acknowledgment that he did not pay federal income taxes for years, has left the American people with considerable gaps in their understanding of the financial dealings.

But this they do know: Mr. Trump will thoroughly reimagine the tone, standards and expectations of the presidency, molding it in his own self-aggrandizing image.

He is set to take the oath of office on Jan. 20.

AMY CHOZICK, ASHLEY PARKER, PATRICK HEALY AND JONATHAN MARTIN CONTRIBUTED REPORTING.

Across the World, Shock and Uncertainty at Trump's Victory

BY THE NEW YORK TIMES | NOV. 9, 2016

THE ELECTION of Donald J. Trump as president of the United States has shocked the world — and has the potential to reshape it.

"I want to tell the world community that while we will always put America's interests first, we will deal fairly with everyone, with everyone — all people and all other nations," Mr. Trump said in his victory speech.

His triumph was seen as good for Russia's president, Vladimir V. Putin, but made some in Mexico nervous.

Leaders from Asia, Europe and Latin America offered congratulations to Mr. Trump or to the United States, but the distinctions in their messages were noteworthy.

SOME ADVICE FROM SOUTH OF THE BORDER

Latin American heads of state wished Mr. Trump well, and offered their own ideas on how he might govern.

Venezuela, a country that Mr. Trump has repeatedly criticized for its leftist leadership, asked Mr. Trump to essentially mind his own country's business by "respecting nonintervention in internal issues and to the right of development and peace."

Juan Manuel Santos, the president of Colombia and Nobel Peace Prize laureate, said he hoped Colombia and the United States "will continue deepening bilateral relations." Mr. Trump has criticized a trade agreement between Colombia and the United States, among many other trade deals.

Álvaro García Linera, Bolivia's leftist vice president, said the voters' endorsement of Mr. Trump's populist message shows how Americans, too, are questioning prevailing economic paradigms in "a passive revolution," this time coming from the right.

Others expressed dismay with the election entirely.

"The excesses of this eccentric millionaire have proven that the number one enemy of the U.S. is not beyond its borders, but rather within," wrote Vladimir Flórez, a Colombian cartoonist popularly known as Vladdo, in El Tiempo newspaper. "This threat called Trump is a product of American society; a nightmarish mutation of the American dream."

ACROSS THE BORDER, APPEALS FOR CALM

Mr. Trump's campaign — and his promise to build a wall on the United States-Mexico border and to deport millions of immigrants in the country illegally — became a rallying point for Mexicans.

He has promised to blow up the North American Free Trade Agreement, or NAFTA, upending commerce between the two countries, valued at about $500 billion a year.

Early on Wednesday — as the peso gyrated — President Enrique Peña Nieto said, "Mexico and the U.S.A. are friends, partners and allies."

Andrés Manuel López Obrador, a popular leftist politician and likely 2018 presidential candidate, asked Mexicans "to remain calm," and said, "We will stay together no matter what the circumstances are."

Foreign Minister Claudia Ruiz Massieu repeated in a television interview on Wednesday morning that Mexico would not pay for the wall.

AZAM AHMED

IN ARGENTINA, CLINTON SUPPORTERS SHIFT GEARS

President Mauricio Macri had rooted for Hillary Clinton but said he hoped to work with Mr. Trump. "One of the issues that worried us is the transition," he said. "We will have to adapt, and that is what we will do."

Earlier in the week, Foreign Minister Susana Malcorra warned that a Trump victory would bring relations between the United States and Argentina "to a standstill," but on Wednesday she praised his "conciliatory" victory speech.

DANIEL POLITI

TRUDEAU AFFIRMS CANADA'S FRIENDSHIP

Prime Minister Justin Trudeau, who enjoys a close relationship with President Obama, said that "Canada has no closer friend, partner and ally than the United States."

He added, "The relationship between our two countries serves as a model for the world."

But Mr. Trump's promise to revisit NAFTA brings unwelcome uncertainty to Canada's economy. Mr. Trudeau's open approach to immigration and refugees is the inverse of Mr. Trump's. And Canada will be in a difficult position if it imposes carbon taxes only to find that Mr. Trump undoes all American efforts to mitigate climate change.

One of the few positive developments for Canada is Mr. Trump's promise to reverse the Obama administration's decision to block the Keystone XL pipeline.

IAN AUSTEN

FROM THE U.N. AND NATO, REMINDERS OF AMERICA'S ROLE

Ban Ki-moon, the United Nations secretary general, said it was "worth recalling and reaffirming that the unity in diversity of the United States is one of the country's greatest strengths."

As if to remind the United States of its role as a guarantor of world stability, he noted that it is "an essential actor across the international agenda."

Mr. Trump has demanded that the NATO allies of the United States foot more of the bill for their collective defense. Jens Stoltenberg, the NATO secretary general, noted that the alliance comes with legal obligations.

"NATO's security guarantee is a treaty commitment and all allies have made a solemn commitment — a solemn commitment — to defend each other," Mr. Stoltenberg said. "We have to remember that the only time that we have invoked Article 5, our collective defense clause, is after an attack on the United States, after 9/11."

RICK GLADSTONE AND JAMES KANTER

ANXIETY IN EUROPE

The two top officials of the European Union — Donald Tusk, president of the European Council, and Jean-Claude Juncker, president of the European Commission — congratulated Mr. Trump and invited him to visit Europe. "Europeans trust that America, whose democratic ideals have always been a beacon of hope around the globe, will continue to invest in its partnerships with friends and allies, to help make our citizens and the people of the world more secure and more prosperous," they wrote.

Later, however, Mr. Tusk, a former prime minister of Poland, warned that Britain's decision to leave the European Union, and the election of Mr. Trump, should raise alarms. "The events of the last months and days should be treated as a warning sign for all who believe in liberal democracy," he said.

Guy Verhofstadt, the leader of a prominent group of lawmakers in the European Parliament and a former prime minister of Belgium, called Mr. Trump's victory "a wake-up call for European leaders," adding, "Donald Trump has declared several times that our priorities are not his."

He added: "We cannot be dependent anymore on the U.S., we have to take charge of our own destiny. Europe should get its act together, too, and set its internal differences aside."

Britain's prime minister, Theresa May, spoke of the country's "enduring and special relationship" with the United States.

President François Hollande of France noted that "some of Donald Trump's campaign positions must be put to the test of the values and the interests that we share with the United States." He added that "disorders in the world are worrying people everywhere, including the people of America, the first world power." The French prime minister, Jean-Marc Ayrault, asked, "What will become of the Paris agreement on the climate, of the nuclear deal with Iran that Donald Trump wants to reconsider?"

Chancellor Angela Merkel congratulated Mr. Trump and offered her cooperation — but stressed that it must rest on human rights and nondiscrimination. Germany's foreign minister, Frank-Walter Steinmeier, said that "if Donald Trump really wants to be president of all Americans, then I think his first duty is to fill in the deep rifts which arose during the campaign."

AURELIEN BREEDEN, JAMES KANTER AND ALISON SMALE

REJOICING FROM FAR-RIGHT LEADERS

Two anti-immigrant nationalist leaders — Geert Wilders in the Netherlands and Marine Le Pen in France — cheered Mr. Trump's victory.

"The Americans are taking their country back," Mr. Wilders, a lawmaker who leads the Party for Freedom and who faces hate-speech charges in his home country, wrote on Twitter. He called Mr. Trump's election "a historic victory" and "a revolution."

Ms. Le Pen, the leader of the National Front in France and a candidate for the French presidency, congratulated Mr. Trump on Twitter and declared the American people "free!" She called it "good news for our country."

Prime Minister Viktor Orban of Hungary, one of the few European leaders who spoke favorably of Mr. Trump during the campaign, wrote on Facebook: "What a great news. Democracy is still alive."

BENOÎT MORENNE AND MARTIN DE BOURMONT

IRAN VOWS TO MAINTAIN NUCLEAR AGREEMENT

Mr. Trump has called the January agreement between Iran and world powers "the worst deal ever," and he has vowed to unilaterally abandon it. Under the agreement, Iran has given up large chunks of its nuclear program in exchange for some sanctions relief.

The head of Iran's atomic energy program told the semiofficial Tasnim news agency on Wednesday that the country would "try to continue to implement the nuclear agreement."

Iran's supreme leader, Ayatollah Ali Khamenei, said last week that the presidential debates had illustrated "the crisis America is in." Some analysts said the election of Mr. Trump was the result of an "awakening," Iran's ideological label for some of the Arab Spring revolts.

One analyst, Farshad Ghorbanpour, who is close to the government of the Iranian president, Hassan Rouhani, said he feared the implications for Mr. Rouhani, who has been promoting better relations with Washington. "Our hard-liners will pressure him, they are very happy now," he said.

THOMAS ERDBRINK

NETANYAHU CALLS TRUMP 'A TRUE FRIEND' OF ISRAEL

"President-elect Trump is a true friend of the State of Israel, and I look forward to working with him to advance security, stability and peace in our region," Prime Minister Benjamin Netanyahu said in a statement. The United States is Israel's most important ally.

The Israeli government, which has often had a tense relationship with the Obama administration, has studiously avoided taking sides, but at the same time, Jerusalem has moved to improve relations with India and Russia, and is in talks to develop economic ties with China.

ISABEL KERSHNER

UNCERTAINTY FOR A MIDDLE EAST ALREADY IN TUMULT

Across the Middle East, where the United States has a long history of often divisive involvement, many seemed to have no idea how to react to the election of Mr. Trump.

President Abdel Fattah el-Sisi of Egypt and Prime Minister Binali Yildirim of Turkey quickly congratulated Mr. Trump, but official reaction was scarce from Saudi Arabia. Mr. Trump said the kingdom may no longer be able to count on American defense guarantees and should give the United States "free oil for the next 10 years."

Syrians, too, said they had little inkling what the vote would mean for the civil war in their country, although many in the opposition had expressed hope that a victory for Hillary Clinton would mean more robust support for the rebels fighting to topple President Bashar al-Assad.

"I am scared, scared for Syria," said Murhaf Jouejati, the chairman of the Day After organization, an independent body that aims to prepare Syrians for a democratic future. "Here is a man who is openly saying that he is going to defer to the Russians on Syria. This is a clear victory for the Assad regime."

Many have expressed worry that Mr. Trump's negative statements about Islam and Muslims would translate into aggressive policies in the region, as well as making it harder for displaced Syrians to seek refuge.

BEN HUBBARD, ANNE BARNARD AND HWAIDA SAAD

IN JAPAN, ANXIETY FROM AN ALLY

Prime Minister Shinzo Abe, who had been planning to meet Mrs. Clinton in Washington in February, tried to calm his country, as the yen surged and stocks stumbled. "Hand in hand with Trump, we will try to work together," he said.

On the campaign trail, Mr. Trump singled out Japan. He claimed that Tokyo was not paying its fair share to support United States military bases, calling into question the American commitment to defend Japan in case of attack.

A rising China could put a check on Mr. Trump's stated ambitions in Asia. "Maybe he will decrease the commitment to Pacific security issues," said Shin Kawashima, professor of international relations at the University of Tokyo. "But if he carries out such a policy, China will be much more authoritative and aggressive in the Pacific. And then most of the alliance countries and security experts in Washington will be against Trump's policies. It is a little difficult for Trump to just change all the old policies."

Mr. Trump's talk of disengaging could embolden Mr. Abe's efforts to build its military capabilities and strengthen ties with Russia.

MOTOKO RICH AND HISAKO UENO

SOUTH KOREA WARNS THE NORTH NOT TO 'MISJUDGE'

President Park Geun-hye of South Korea instructed her government to coordinate closely with Mr. Trump's transition team to ensure that her country and the United States would maintain sanctions and pressure on North Korea to stop its nuclear weapons program.

"North Korea should not misjudge the solidity of our alliance with the United States and our joint ability to respond" to provocations, said Jeong Joon-hee, a government spokesman.

Mr. Trump unsettled South Koreans when he said that he might withdraw American troops from their country unless Seoul paid more for their presence. He also indicated that he might let Japan and South Korea protect themselves with nuclear weapons and that he might negotiate directly with the North Korean leader, Kim Jong-un.

Mr. Trump's surprisingly strong performance caught analysts off guard, but it was welcome news for those in South Korea who believe that their country must build its own nuclear weapons to defend against North Korea.

CHOE SANG-HUN

IN SOUTHEAST ASIA, TWO LEADERS BACK TRUMP

Prime Minister Najib Razak of Malaysia was one of the first leaders to offer effusive praise for Mr. Trump.

"The world has watched this year's presidential election with fascination," he said in a statement. "At almost every turn, media commentators have been proved wrong and the results anticipated by experts have been overturned. Donald Trump was considered a distant outsider when his candidacy was first announced. He beat the establishment consensus by winning the Republican nomination, and did so again with his remarkable victory today. Mr. Trump's success shows that politicians should never take voters for granted."

Mr. Najib, who has stared down corruption charges, added, "His appeal to Americans who have been left behind — those who want to see their government more focused on their interests and welfare, and less embroiled in foreign interventions that proved to be against U.S. interests — have won Mr. Trump the White House."

Arriving in Malaysia on Wednesday evening, Rodrigo Duterte, the president of the Philippines, who has lashed out at the United States and at Mr. Obama in often profane comments, mentioned Mr. Trump in a speech to overseas Filipino workers.

"Congratulations," he said. "We are alike. We both swear."

SEWELL CHAN AND RICHARD C. PADDOCK

A SURPRISE FOR THE WORLD'S LARGEST DEMOCRACY

Prime Minister Narendra Modi said in a tweet addressed at Mr. Trump, "We appreciate the friendship you have articulated towards India during your campaign."

For India, a central question is whether Washington will reduce its military presence.

"If that is called into question, India will no longer be able to rely on the U.S. to be there as a security provider," said Dhruva Jaishankar, a fellow at the Brookings Institution India Center. The result could be more assertive attitudes from China, Japan and Korea.

Manjeet Kripalani, the executive director of Gateway House, a Mumbai-based think tank, likened Mr. Trump to Putin of Russia, President Recep Tayyip Erdogan of Turkey, and Mr. Modi. (A former journalist, Ms. Kripalani worked for Steve Forbes's 1996 presidential campaign.)

As far as any change in the relationship between India and the United States is concerned, she predicted, "You will find the Trump administration being realistic about Pakistan, being realistic about India and realistic about China."

ELLEN BARRY AND NIDA NAJAR

AUSTRALIA SAYS U.S. HAS 'NO BETTER FRIEND'

Prime Minister Malcolm Turnbull reassured his people that "Americans understand that they have no stronger ally, no better friend, than Australia."

Mr. Turnbull said the American role in the Pacific region had underpinned stability, economic growth and a rules-based order, a term he and Foreign Minister Julie Bishop have used when discussing the resolution of disputes with China over territorial and fishing rights in the South China Sea.

"I have great confidence that all of our engagement will continue to be strong and intimate, filled with the trust and confidence that has characterized it for so many years," Mr. Turnbull said.

MICHELLE INNIS

Uncertainty Over Donald Trump's Foreign Policy Risks Global Instability

BY MAX FISHER | NOV. 9, 2016

WHETHER OR NOT Donald J. Trump follows through on his campaign pledges to diminish or possibly abandon American commitments to security alliances such as NATO, his election victory forces nations around the world to begin preparing for the day they can no longer count on the American-backed order.

This creates a danger that derives less from Mr. Trump's words, which are often inconsistent or difficult to parse, than from the inability to predict his actions or how other states might respond to them.

That uncertainty puts pressure on allies and adversaries alike to position themselves, before Mr. Trump even takes office, for a world that could be on the verge of losing one of its longest-standing pillars of stability.

"You're going to see a lot of fear among America's allies, and in some cases they may try to do something about it," said James Goldgeier, a political scientist and the dean of American University's School of International Service.

Mr. Trump's election comes at a moment when rising powers are already pushing against the American-led order: China in Asia, Iran in the Middle East, and particularly Vladimir V. Putin's Russia in Europe.

Those powers will be tempted to test their new limits.

Allies in Europe or Asia, suddenly considering the prospect of facing a hostile power alone, cannot wait to see whether Mr. Trump means what he says, Mr. Goldgeier said, adding that they "will have to start making alternate plans now."

Western European states like Germany and France "may decide they can no longer afford to take a tough stand against Putin's Russia," he suggested. "They may decide their best bet is to cut some kind

ERIC THAYER FOR THE NEW YORK TIMES

Donald J. Trump, in Virginia Beach, Va., in September 2016.

of deal with him," even if it means tolerating Russian influence over Eastern Europe.

Or they may not. But that possibility — and the fact that Eastern European states may have to worry, and plan accordingly — shows how uncertainty can build on itself, adding instability to already tumultuous regions.

Over the past year, I have been asking policy experts to evaluate Mr. Trump's likely foreign policy, and they have consistently given me the same answer: They are unable to stitch Mr. Trump's rambling speeches and scant white papers into a coherent worldview.

That lack of clarity seemed purely academic when polls predicted a sweeping victory for his rival, Hillary Clinton.

Now, it is a problem shared by world leaders, friendly and unfriendly, who had long planned their foreign policies around the role reliably played by the United States.

Instead, countries must prepare for a very unfamiliar world, one whose most powerful nation and global guarantor is no longer so easy to predict. Even if they believe that the United States-led order will most likely remain, they have little choice but to hedge against its disintegration — acting as if the world had already returned to a bygone era of shifting alliances and regional spheres of power.

The difficulty of predicting Mr. Trump's foreign policy could create other forms of destabilizing uncertainty.

Asked about the international agreement to restrict Iran's nuclear program, Daryl G. Kimball, director of the Arms Control Association, said it was unclear to him — and most likely to Middle Eastern leaders — whether Mr. Trump "would deliberately or inadvertently take actions that unravel that agreement."

Because Middle Eastern countries would so struggle to predict or plan around Mr. Trump's Iran policies, and because he seems thus far unlikely to win over European leaders whom he has insulted from the campaign trail, Mr. Kimball said, "the future of the Iran deal is now in greater jeopardy."

Critics See Stephen Bannon, Trump's Pick for Strategist, as Voice of Racism

BY MICHAEL D. SHEAR, MAGGIE HABERMAN AND MICHAEL S. SCHMIDT | NOV. 14, 2016

WASHINGTON — A fierce chorus of critics denounced President-elect Donald J. Trump on Monday for appointing Stephen K. Bannon, a nationalist media mogul, to a top White House position, even as President Obama described Mr. Trump as "pragmatic," not ideological, and held out hope that he would rise to the challenge of the presidency.

"It's important for us to let him make his decisions," Mr. Obama said. "The American people will judge over the course of the next couple of years whether they like what they see."

Mr. Obama's conciliatory remarks disappointed supporters who had hoped that he would add his voice to the criticism of the president-elect for naming Mr. Bannon as his chief strategist. Civil rights groups, senior Democrats and some Republican strategists have assailed Mr. Trump, saying that Mr. Bannon, the former head of Breitbart News, will bring anti-Semitic, nationalist and racist views to the West Wing.

In the midst of the furor over Mr. Bannon's appointment, Rudolph W. Giuliani, the former mayor of New York City, emerged as a leading candidate to be secretary of state, according to people familiar with the deliberations in the 26th-floor office in Trump Tower where Mr. Trump was ensconced throughout the day. That would make Mr. Giuliani, a contentious former prosecutor, the president's emissary to a turbulent world.

There has been intense jockeying among several of Mr. Trump's highest-profile campaign advisers, suggesting a competition to lead the new administration's foreign policy, national security and crime-fighting agencies. Mr. Trump is also considering naming Mr. Giuliani or Senator Jeff Sessions of Alabama as the next attorney general,

DAMON WINTER/THE NEW YORK TIMES

Stephen Bannon, left, in Grand Rapids, Mich. for Donald Trump's final campaign event.

according to the people familiar with the discussions.

But Mr. Giuliani said Monday night at a Wall Street Journal election forum that he would not be going to the Justice Department. And if Mr. Sessions, a relentless critic of illegal immigration, is nominated for attorney general, he can expect opponents to bring up the fact that he was once rejected for a federal judgeship after officials testified that he had made racist comments.

Mr. Giuliani seems more eager to be secretary of state, though John R. Bolton, a fierce foreign policy hawk who served as ambassador to the United Nations and under secretary of state under President George W. Bush, is also under consideration, the people familiar with the discussions said. Richard Grenell, who was Mr. Bolton's spokesman at the United Nations, is being considered as ambassador there.

People with knowledge of the process described a series of chaotic discussions and said Mr. Trump might also choose Mr. Giuliani or Mr. Sessions to lead the Department of Homeland Security, though neither has expressed interest in that job.

RUTH FREMSON/THE NEW YORK TIMES

Kellyanne Conway, a key Trump adviser.

In 1986, before Mr. Sessions became a senator himself, a Republican-controlled Senate rejected his nomination by President Ronald Reagan to a federal judgeship. Several United States attorneys testified that he had made racist comments, including calling an African-American lawyer "boy," and that he had been hostile to civil rights cases. Mr. Sessions denied making most of the remarks, but apologized for once saying that he had thought the Ku Klux Klan was O.K. until he heard that some members smoked pot; he called it a joke.

As for Mr. Bolton, he was known in the Bush administration for his conservative and sometimes confrontational views. Before his nomination as United Nations ambassador, he once said of the 38-story United Nations building in New York, "If it lost 10 stories, it wouldn't make a bit of difference."

If named to Mr. Trump's cabinet, Mr. Bolton could clash with the president on Russia: He has accused the Obama administration of being weak in that area and recently wrote in favor of NATO membership for Ukraine, a move that would infuriate Moscow. Mr. Trump spoke by telephone on Monday with President Vladimir V. Putin of Russia, and according to a statement released by the Kremlin, the two men agreed "on the absolutely unsatisfactory state of bilateral relations" and vowed to improve them.

Aides to Mr. Trump declined to comment on reports of the leading contenders for cabinet posts. But Kellyanne Conway, a top adviser, defended Mr. Bannon in brief remarks to reporters in New York, describing him as the "general of this campaign" and saying that "people should look at the full résumé."

"He has got a Harvard business degree. He's a naval officer. He has success in entertainment," Ms. Conway said, calling him a "brilliant tactician."

Ms. Conway denied that Mr. Bannon had a connection to right-wing nationalists or that he would bring those views to the White House. "I'm personally offended that you think I would manage a campaign where that would be one of the going philosophies," she said.

Mr. Bannon has said that while there are fringe elements associated with the right-wing nationalist movement, his critics are painting with too broad a brush.

"These people are patriots," he said. "They love their country. They just want their country taken care of."

Even as Mr. Trump works to fill his administration, his team has yet to begin the real work of transitioning to the helm of the government because they have not completed the necessary paperwork.

White House officials said Monday that Gov. Chris Christie of New Jersey, who was in charge of Mr. Trump's transition team until Friday, had signed a memorandum of understanding that ensured confidentiality. But Mr. Christie was dismissed on Friday and replaced by Vice President-elect Mike Pence, invalidating the agreement and leaving the transition process in a state of suspended animation.

At a news conference before leaving on a weeklong trip to Greece, Germany and Peru, Mr. Obama appeared to be doing his best to give

Mr. Trump space as he begins forming his administration. The president also continued his efforts to persuade Mr. Trump to preserve his legacy, pointedly reminding him that repealing the Affordable Care Act could be politically unpopular and that ripping up global agreements like the Iran nuclear deal or the Paris climate accord would be difficult.

Mr. Obama refused to say whether he still considered Mr. Trump unfit to sit in the Oval Office and have access to the nuclear codes, and equated Mr. Trump's shortcomings with his own troubles organizing paperwork on his desk. The closest he came to criticizing Mr. Trump was when he said the president-elect would have to temper his impulses to make explosive comments and lie once he was sworn in.

"There are going to be certain elements of his temperament that will not serve him well unless he recognizes them and corrects them," Mr. Obama said. "I think he recognizes that this is different, and so do the American people."

Congressional Republicans remained largely silent about the appointment of Mr. Bannon, choosing instead to praise Mr. Trump's choice of Reince Priebus, the chairman of the Republican National Committee, as the new White House chief of staff. In remarks to reporters, Representative Kevin McCarthy of California, the Republican majority leader in the House, said he would "not prejudge" Mr. Trump's choice.

But critics of Mr. Bannon continued to raise questions about his background and his tenure as the chairman of Breitbart News. A 2011 radio interview surfaced in which Mr. Bannon praised Ann Coulter, Michele Bachmann and Sarah Palin by saying they were not "a bunch of dykes that came from the Seven Sisters schools up in New England."

"That drives the left insane," he added, "and that's why they hate these women."

The Council on American-Islamic Relations said the selection of Mr. Bannon "sends the disturbing message that anti-Muslim conspiracy theories and white nationalist ideology will be welcome in the White House."

That view was echoed by the Southern Poverty Law Center, which tracks hate groups and said Mr. Trump "should rescind this hire."

"In his victory speech, Trump said he intended to be president for 'all Americans,' " the center said. "Bannon should go."

Republicans who had long opposed Mr. Trump's candidacy also took to Twitter on Sunday night and Monday morning to warn that his choice to rely on the advice of Mr. Bannon was an indication of the way he would govern.

"The racist, fascist extreme right is represented footsteps from the Oval Office," said John Weaver, a Republican strategist who ran the presidential campaign of Gov. John Kasich of Ohio and previously advised Senator John McCain of Arizona. "Be very vigilant, America."

But people close to Mr. Bannon came to his defense. Joel B. Pollak, an author and editor at Breitbart, called him an "American patriot who also defends Israel and has deep empathy for the Jewish people."

Jewish leaders and supporters of Israel expressed alarm at Mr. Bannon's appointment, pointing to anti-Semitic writings on the Breitbart website.

"In his roles as editor of the Breitbart website and as a strategist in the Trump campaign, Mr. Bannon was responsible for the advancement of ideologies antithetical to our nation, including anti-Semitism, misogyny, racism and Islamophobia," said Rabbi Jonah Dov Pesner, the director of the Religious Action Center of Reform Judaism. "There should be no place for such views in the White House."

Mike Huckabee, the former governor of Arkansas, accused Mr. Bannon's critics of sour grapes. On Twitter, he wrote that Mr. Bannon should embrace the criticism from the Council on American-Islamic Relations, or CAIR.

"Critics of Steve Bannon know he's smarter and tougher than they are," Mr. Huckabee wrote. "When CAIR doesn't like you, that is a good thing."

At Conference, Political Consultants Wonder Where They Went Wrong

BY JULIE TURKEWITZ | NOV. 14, 2016

DENVER — At the governor's mansion here on Friday, past the columned entryway and the French chandeliers, Emmy Ruiz placed a hand on the shoulder of a fellow Hillary Clinton operative. "It's like we're at a funeral," said Ms. Ruiz, dressed — perhaps coincidentally — in black.

Just days after Donald J. Trump's surprise presidential victory, the nation's professional political forecasters and persuaders — the pollsters, the ad creators, the campaign strategists — gathered in Denver for their annual convention. It was supposed to be a celebration of big data and strategic wizardry for a multibillion-dollar industry that has spent nearly a century packaging political candidates.

NICK COTE FOR THE NEW YORK TIMES

Political consultants and pollsters unwinding at a reception during an International Association of Political Consultants conference in Denver.

Instead, the conference of the International Association of Political Consultants felt like a therapy session for a business in psychological free fall.

"I need to make sure I state this very clearly so that nobody thinks that I feel otherwise: I got this really wrong," Chris Anderson, a Democratic pollster who had predicted a Clinton win, said during a session before the gathering at the governor's mansion. "We're going to continue to learn from Donald Trump how to effectively message," he said. "Because he can do it really well."

The business of political consulting was born, many say, in 1933 when the newspaper writers Clem Whitaker and Leone Baxter were hired to defeat Upton Sinclair in his antipoverty bid for governor of California. (When Sinclair lost, he blamed the defeat on a "staff of political chemists.")

The industry has since evolved into a sophisticated army of data analysts, message crafters and others whose firms turn billions of dollars given to candidates and their surrogates into services. Television advertisements. Email lists. Get-out-the-vote strategies.

But everything about this election seemed to throw into question the value of those tactics — and even of the consultants themselves. In the end, Mrs. Clinton's battalion of advisers was defeated by a wild, seemingly unchoreographed candidate who, according to the most recent data, spent more money on shirts, hats, signs and similar items than on field consulting, voter lists and data.

Over the weekend, 150 or so participants moved between a high-ceilinged conference room at the Westin hotel and other activities, including the reception at the governor's mansion and a dinner at an adobe fort in the foothills of the Rocky Mountains. (Organizers nixed a tour of a marijuana grow house after too many people expressed interest.)

In one session dedicated to polling, three panelists who had predicted Mrs. Clinton would win took to the stage, framed by a royal blue backdrop. Instead of PowerPoint presentations and state-by-

NICK COTE FOR THE NEW YORK TIMES

Chris Anderson, a Democratic pollster, at the International Association of Political Consultants gathering.

state voter analyses, there was morose self-flagellation, as some admitted they had spent the election seduced by "magical thinking," unable to envision a Trump presidency and therefore blind to the story in front of them.

Margie Omero of PSB Research theorized that pollsters had held back Trump-leaning data, unwilling to release something that looked like an outlier. Or that Trump supporters had simply not told pollsters the truth, either embarrassed by their choice or angry at callers whom they perceived as part of a conspiracy against him.

"It was impossible to conceive of an incoming President Trump," said Ms. Omero, whose firm has worked for both former President Bill Clinton and Hillary Clinton over the years. "A couple-point advantage seemed comforting to prevent something so catastrophic."

Mr. Anderson, the Democratic pollster, said he should have seen the win all along.

"The story that played out was right in front of me," he said. (Mrs. Clinton never went above 45 percent in his surveys.) "But my basic assumption, and why I think why I was wrong was I continued to say to myself: 'This segment of voters, about 15 percent, who view both of them unfavorably, they think Clinton has the judgment, temperament and qualifications to be president. They do not think the same of Trump.' So I believed that at the end of the day they would vote for Clinton."

It appears they did not.

In one of the more raucous portions of the conference, consultants assembled for a post-mortem session on campaign strategy. Onstage were Ms. Ruiz, who ran Mrs. Clinton's operation in Colorado, and Rich Pelletier, a deputy campaign manager for Senator Bernie Sanders of Vermont, whom Mrs. Clinton faced in the Democratic primary race. Between them was Wayne Allyn Root, a Trump adviser wearing a pin-stripe suit, a red tie and a very, very broad smile.

"He was going to win from the beginning. Nobody got it. And I got it. I knew it," Mr. Root said, describing a campaign strategy based more on gut and anecdote than science. "No matter how bad the polls look, they are meaningless because the anger and volatility of this electorate does not show up in the polls. My people are not telling the pollster they're for Donald Trump."

His presentation was met with grumbles, then shouts, and finally calls from an audience of angered consultants. "It's rigged! It's rigged!"

Firings and Discord Put Trump Transition Team in a State of Disarray

BY JULIE HIRSCHFELD DAVIS, MARK MAZZETTI AND MAGGIE HABERMAN | NOV. 15, 2016

WASHINGTON — President-elect Donald J. Trump's transition was in disarray on Tuesday, marked by firings, infighting and revelations that American allies were blindly dialing in to Trump Tower to try to reach the soon-to-be-leader of the free world.

One week after Mr. Trump scored an upset victory that took him by surprise, his team was improvising the most basic traditions of assuming power. That included working without official State Department briefing materials in his first conversations with foreign leaders.

Two officials who had been handling national security for the transition, former Representative Mike Rogers of Michigan and Matthew Freedman, a lobbyist who consults with corporations and foreign governments, were fired. Both were part of what officials described as a purge orchestrated by Jared Kushner, Mr. Trump's son-in-law and close adviser.

The dismissals followed the abrupt firing on Friday of Gov. Chris Christie of New Jersey, who was replaced as chief of the transition by Vice President-elect Mike Pence. Mr. Kushner, a transition official said, was systematically dismissing people like Mr. Rogers who had ties with Mr. Christie. As a federal prosecutor, Mr. Christie had sent Mr. Kushner's father to jail.

Prominent American allies were in the meantime scrambling to figure out how and when to contact Mr. Trump. At times, they have been patched through to him in his luxury office tower with little warning, according to a Western diplomat who spoke on the condition of anonymity to detail private conversations.

President Abdel Fattah el-Sisi of Egypt was the first to reach Mr. Trump for such a call last Wednesday, followed by Prime Minister

Benjamin Netanyahu of Israel not long afterward. But that was about 24 hours before Prime Minister Theresa May of Britain got through — a striking break from diplomatic practice given the close alliance between the United States and Britain.

Despite the haphazard nature of Mr. Trump's early calls with world leaders, his advisers said the transition team was not suffering unusual setbacks. They argued that they were hard at work behind the scenes dealing with the same troubles that incoming presidents have faced for decades.

And Mr. Trump himself fired back at critics with a Twitter message he sent about 10 p.m. "Very organized process taking place as I decide on Cabinet and many other positions," he wrote. "I am the only one who knows who the finalists are!"

The process is "completely normal," said Rudolph W. Giuliani, the former New York mayor, who emerged on Tuesday as the leading contender to be Mr. Trump's secretary of state. "It happened in the Reagan transition. Clinton had delays in hiring people."

Mr. Giuliani, who made his comments in a telephone interview, added: "This is a hard thing to do. Transitions always have glitches. This is an enormously complex process."

There were some reports within the transition of score-settling.

One member of the transition team said that at least one reason Mr. Rogers had fallen out of favor among Mr. Trump's advisers was that, as chairman of the House Intelligence Committee, he had overseen a report about the 2012 attacks on the American diplomatic compound in Benghazi, Libya, which concluded that the Obama administration had not intentionally misled the public about the events there. That report echoed the findings of numerous other government investigations into the episode.

The report's conclusions were at odds with the campaign position of Mr. Trump, who repeatedly blamed Hillary Clinton, his Democratic opponent and the secretary of state during the attacks, for the resulting deaths of four Americans.

Eliot A. Cohen, a former State Department official who had criticized Mr. Trump during the campaign but said after his election that he would keep an open mind about advising him, said Tuesday on Twitter that he had changed his opinion. After speaking to the transition team, he wrote, he had "changed my recommendation: stay away."

He added: "They're angry, arrogant, screaming 'you LOST!' Will be ugly."

Mr. Cohen, a conservative Republican who served under President George W. Bush, said Trump transition officials had excoriated him after he offered some names of people who might serve in the new administration, but only if they felt departments were led by credible people.

"They think of these jobs as lollipops," Mr. Cohen said in an interview.

Senator John McCain, Republican of Arizona and the chairman of the Senate Armed Services Committee, weighed in as well. On Tuesday, he issued a blunt warning to Mr. Trump and his emerging foreign policy team not to be taken in by President Vladimir V. Putin of Russia, whom Mr. Trump praised during the campaign.

"The Obama administration's last attempt at resetting relations with Russia culminated in Putin's invasion of Ukraine and military intervention in the Middle East," Mr. McCain said.

Some of the early transition difficulties may reflect the fact that Mr. Trump, who has no governing experience or Washington network and campaigned as an agent of change, does not have a long list of establishment figures from the Bush era to tap. His allies suggested that might ultimately prove positive for Mr. Trump if he was able to assemble a functioning team that would bring new perspectives to his administration.

For advice on building Mr. Trump's national security team, his inner circle has been relying on three hawkish current and former American officials: Representative Devin Nunes, Republican of California, who is chairman of the House Intelligence Committee; Peter

Hoekstra, a former Republican congressman and former chairman of the Intelligence Committee; and Frank Gaffney, a Pentagon official during the Reagan administration and a founder of the Center for Security Policy.

Mr. Gaffney has long advanced baseless conspiracy theories, including that President Obama might be a closet Muslim. The Southern Poverty Law Center described him as "one of America's most notorious Islamophobes."

Prominent donors to Mr. Trump were also having little success in recruiting people for rank-and-file posts in his administration.

Rebekah Mercer, the scion of a powerful family of conservative donors and a member of Mr. Trump's executive transition committee, has said in conversations with Republican operatives and previous administration officials that she was having trouble finding takers for posts at the under secretary level and below, according to a person familiar with her outreach efforts. She told them that the transition team was more than a month behind schedule and on a tight timeline.

In another delay, Mr. Pence did not sign legally required paperwork to allow his team to begin collaborating with Mr. Obama's aides until Tuesday evening, a transition spokesman said. Mr. Christie on Election Day signed a memorandum of understanding to put the process into motion as soon as the outcome was determined, but once he was ousted from the job, Mr. Pence had to sign a new agreement.

The paperwork serves as a nondisclosure agreement for both sides, ensuring that members of the president-elect's team do not divulge information about the inner workings of the government.

Teams throughout the federal government that have prepared briefing materials and reports for the incoming president's team are on standby, waiting to begin passing the information to counterparts on Mr. Trump's staff.

As of Tuesday afternoon, officials at key agencies including the Justice and Defense Departments said they had received no contact from the president-elect's team.

Inside a Fake News Sausage Factory: 'This Is All About Income'

BY ANDREW HIGGINS, MIKE MCINTIRE AND GABRIEL J.X. DANCE | NOV. 25, 2016

TBILISI, GEORGIA — Jobless and with graduation looming, a computer science student at the premier university in the nation of Georgia decided early this year that money could be made from America's voracious appetite for passionately partisan political news. He set up a website, posted gushing stories about Hillary Clinton and waited for ad sales to soar.

"I don't know why, but it did not work," said the student, Beqa Latsabidze, 22, who was savvy enough to change course when he realized what did drive traffic: laudatory stories about Donald J. Trump that mixed real — and completely fake — news in a stew of anti-Clinton fervor.

More than 6,000 miles away in Vancouver, a Canadian who runs a satirical website, John Egan, had made a similar observation. Mr. Egan's site, The Burrard Street Journal, offers sendups of the news, not fake news, and he is not trying to fool anyone. But he, too, discovered that writing about Mr. Trump was a "gold mine." His traffic soared and his work, notably a story that President Obama would move to Canada if Mr. Trump won, was plundered by Mr. Latsabidze and other internet entrepreneurs for their own websites.

"It's all Trump," Mr. Egan said by telephone. "People go nuts for it."

With Mr. Obama now warning of the corrosive threat from fake political news circulated on Facebook and other social media, the pressing question is who produces these stories, and how does this overheated, often fabricated news ecosystem work?

Some analysts worry that foreign intelligence agencies are meddling in American politics and using fake news to influence elections. But one window into how the meat in fake sausages gets ground can be found in the buccaneering internet economy, where satire produced in

Canada can be taken by a recent college graduate in the former Soviet republic of Georgia and presented as real news to attract clicks from credulous readers in the United States. Mr. Latsabidze said his only incentive was to make money from Google ads by luring people off Facebook pages and onto his websites.

To gin up material, Mr. Latsabidze often simply cut and pasted, sometimes massaging headlines but mostly just copying material from elsewhere, including Mr. Egan's prank story on Mr. Obama. Mr. Egan was not amused to see his satirical work on Mr. Latsabidze's website and filed a copyright infringement notice to defend his intellectual property.

Yet Mr. Egan conceded a certain professional glee that Mr. Trump is here to stay. "Now that we've got him for four years," he said, "I can't believe it."

By some estimates, bogus news stories appearing online and on social media had an even greater reach in the final months of the presidential campaign than articles by mainstream news organizations.

SOUL SEARCHING

Since then, internet giants like Facebook and Google have engaged in soul searching over their roles in disseminating false news. Google announced that it would ban websites that host fake news from using its online advertising service, while Facebook's chief executive, Mark Zuckerberg, outlined some of the options his company was considering, including simpler ways for users to flag suspicious content.

In Tbilisi, the two-room rented apartment Mr. Latsabidze shares with his younger brother is an unlikely offshore outpost of America's fake news industry. The two brothers, both computer experts, get help from a third young Georgian, an architect.

They say they have no keen interest in politics themselves and initially placed bets across the American political spectrum and experimented with show business news, too. They set up a pro-Clinton website, walkwithher.com, a Facebook page cheering Bernie Sanders and a web digest of straightforward political news plagiarized from The New York Times and other mainstream news media.

But those sites, among the more than a dozen registered by Mr. Latsabidze, were busts. Then he shifted all his energy to Mr. Trump. His flagship pro-Trump website, departed.co, gained remarkable traction in a crowded field in the prelude to the Nov. 8 election thanks to steady menu of relentlessly pro-Trump and anti-Clinton stories. (On Wednesday, a few hours after The New York Times met with Mr. Latsabidze to ask him about his activities, the site vanished along with his Facebook page.)

"My audience likes Trump," he said. "I don't want to write bad things about Trump. If I write fake stories about Trump, I lose my audience."

Some of his Trump stories are true, some are highly slanted and others are totally false, like one this summer reporting that "the Mexican government announced they will close their borders to Americans in the event that Donald Trump is elected President of the United States." Data compiled by Buzzfeed showed that the story was the third most-trafficked fake story on Facebook from May to July.

So successful was the formula that others in Georgia and other faraway lands joined in, too, including Nika Kurdadze, a college acquaintance of Mr. Latsabidze's who set up his own pro-Trump site, newsbreakshere.com. Its recent offerings included a fake report headlined: "Stop it Liberals…Hillary Lost the Popular Vote by Several Million. Here's Why." That story, like most of Mr. Latsabidze's work, was pilfered from the web.

Mr. Latsabidze initially ran into no problems from all his cutting and pasting of other people's stories, and he even got ripped off himself when a rival in India hijacked a pro-Trump Facebook page he had set up to drive traffic to his websites. (He said that the Indian rival had offered $10,000 to buy the page, but that he had reneged on payment after being provided with access rights and commandeered it for himself.)

Then the notice arrived from Mr. Egan in Canada, which prompted the company that hosts Mr. Latsabidze's websites, including departed.co, to shut them down for two days until he removed the offending story.

"It was really bad for me," Mr. Latsabidze recalled. "Traffic dropped and I had to start everything all over again."

Mr. Egan, for his part, said he did not like others making money unfairly off his labor. And he estimated that "probably half" the readers of his stories believe they are true because of the widespread theft by other websites.

"A lot of that was conservative readers who see it picked up on other sites and believe it," Mr. Egan said. "In many cases, they haven't actually read it, they're just reacting to a headline."

FORM OF INFOTAINMENT

Mr. Latsabidze said he was amazed that anyone could mistake many of the articles he posts for real news, insisting they are simply a form of infotainment that should not be taken too seriously.

"I don't call it fake news; I call it satire," he said. He avoids sex and violence because they violate Facebook rules, he said, but he sees nothing wrong otherwise with providing readers with what they want.

"Nobody really believes that Mexico is going to close its border," he said, sipping coffee this week in a McDonald's in downtown Tbilisi. "This is crazy."

All the same, the Mexico-closing-its-border story proved so popular after it appeared on his site that he hunted around on the web for other articles on the same theme. He found a tall tale about Mexico planning to call back its citizens from the United States if Mr. Trump won. This, too, generated huge traffic, though not quite as much as the first one, which Mr. Latsabidze described as "a really great story."

He insisted he has nothing against Mexicans or Muslims, whose exclusion from the United States is requested by an online petition that often appears on his websites and who are invariably presented in a negative light in the stories he posts.

"I am not against Muslims," he said. "I just saw that there was interest. They are in the news." Nor, he added, is he particularly against Mrs. Clinton, though he personally prefers Mr. Trump.

If his pro-Clinton site had taken off, he said, he would have pressed on with that, but "people did not engage," so he focused on serving pro-Trump supporters instead. They, he quickly realized, were a far more receptive audience "because they are angry" and eager to read outrageous tales.

"For me, this is all about income, nothing more," he added.

The income comes mostly from Google, which pays a few cents each time a reader sees or clicks on advertisements embedded in one of Mr. Latsabidze's websites. His best month, which coincided with the hit bogus story about Mexico closing the border, brought in around $6,000, though monthly revenue is usually much lower.

Mr. Obama, speaking in Berlin last week, assailed the spread of phony news on Facebook and other platforms, warning that "if we are not serious about facts and what's true and what's not" and "if we can't discriminate between serious arguments and propaganda, then we have problems."

While Facebook does not directly provide Mr. Latsabidze any revenue, it plays a central role in driving traffic to his websites. He initially established several fake Facebook pages intended to steer traffic to his websites, including one supposedly set up by a beautiful woman named Valkiara Beka. This woman, he acknowledged, does not really exist. "She is me," he said.

He discovered, however, that such pages were ineffective compared with legitimate Facebook pages from real people, particularly Trump supporters, because they have so much energy and love promoting stories they like.

Departed.co — named after Mr. Latsabidze's favorite movie, "The Departed," and recently redirected to usatodaycom.com — published dozens of stories daily, many of them similar to one posted on Nov. 17 with the headline, "This Is Huuge! International Arrest Warrant Issued

By Putin For George Soros!" The story was not true and had already been published on scores of other fake news sites around the web.

Then there are the stories that have a grain of truth, along with big dollops of exaggeration and extrapolation, like "Dying Hillary Says She Just Wants To Curl Up And Never Leave Her House Again After Defeat." Mrs. Clinton did say the day after her election defeat that she just wanted to curl up with a book. But she was not, as far as anyone knows, dying.

KREMLIN SUSPICIONS

In the prelude to the election, bogus reports about Mrs. Clinton's health and highly favorable ones about Mr. Trump were promoted with gusto by Russian state-controlled news media outlets and legions of pro-Russian internet agitators. This has stirred suspicions that the Kremlin has had a hand in the fake news industry, prompting American researchers to assert in recent studies that the online blurring of the boundary between truth and falsehood is in part the result of Russian manipulation.

But Mr. Latsabidze and others here say they serve only their bank balances, not Russia or anything else.

He insisted that his team operated entirely on its own and that it did not want or need outside help. He said that it took him just two hours to set up a basic website and that anyone with a modicum of computer savvy could quickly start hawking news — real or fake — online.

"I did not invent anything," he said. "It has all been done before."

Mr. Latsabidze, who apparently has broken no laws, said that any crackdown on fake news might work in the short term but that "something else will come along to replace it."

"If they want to, they can control everything," he said, "but this will stop freedom of speech."

For now, the postelection period has been bad for business, with a sharp fall in the appetite for incendiary political news favoring Mr. Trump. Traffic to departed.co and affiliated websites has plunged in recent weeks by at least 50 percent, Mr. Latsabidze said.

"If Hillary had won, it would be better for us," he said. "I could write about the bad things she was going to do," he said. "I did not write to make Trump win. I just wanted to get viewers and make some money."

In the months since he got into the fake news business, Mr. Latsabidze has landed a day job as a programmer with a software company, which he sees as a better future. "This is more stable work," he said.

But he seemed reluctant to quit altogether.

"Are there any elections coming up in the U.K.?" Mr. Latsabidze asked.

He was disappointed to hear that none were scheduled soon. But, advised that France will hold a hotly contested presidential election next April featuring a Trump-like candidate in the form of Marine Le Pen, a far-right populist, he perked up.

"Maybe I should learn some French," he said.

Donald Trump Rode to Power in the Role of the Common Man

BY ALEXANDER BURNS | NOV. 9, 2016

DONALD JOHN TRUMP defied the skeptics who said he would never run, and the political veterans who scoffed at his slapdash campaign.

He attacked the norms of American politics, singling out groups for derision on the basis of race and religion and attacking the legitimacy of the political process.

He ignored conventions of common decency, employing casual vulgarity and raining personal humiliation on his political opponents and critics in the media.

And in the ultimate act of defiance, Mr. Trump emerged victorious, summoning a tidal wave of support from less educated whites displaced by changes in the economy and deeply resistant to the country's shifting cultural and racial tones. In his triumph, Mr. Trump has

ERIC THAYER FOR THE NEW YORK TIMES

Donald J. Trump summoned a tidal wave of support from whites feeling displaced by economic changes.

delivered perhaps the greatest shock to the American political system in modern times and opened the door to an era of extraordinary political uncertainty at home and around the globe.

The slashing, freewheeling campaign that took him to the doorstep of the White House replicated a familiar pattern from Mr. Trump's life, but on an Olympian scale.

The son of a wealthy real estate developer in Queens, Mr. Trump, 70, spent decades pursuing social acceptance in upscale Manhattan and seeking, at times desperately, to persuade the wider world to see him as a great man of affairs. But Mr. Trump was often met with scoffing disdain by wealthy elites and mainstream civic leaders, culminating in a mortifying roast by President Obama at the White House Correspondents Dinner in 2011.

So Mr. Trump fashioned himself instead as a proudly garish champion of the common man — a person of unsophisticated tastes but distinctive popular appeal — and acted the part in extravagant fashion, first in the New York tabloids and then on national television. He became a pundit of sorts, fulminating against crime in New York City and international trade and Mr. Obama's legitimacy as president, often in racially incendiary terms.

His candidacy unfolded in much the same way: as the rampage of an aggrieved outsider, aligned more with the cultural sensibilities of blue-collar whites than with his peers in society.

On the first day of his run — June 16, 2015 — Mr. Trump drew a direct parallel between his determined quest for success in New York and his entry into the political arena.

Addressing a crowd made up largely of reporters in the atrium of Trump Tower, Mr. Trump noted that political seers had predicted, "He'll never run." Seconds later, he mused that his father, Fred Trump, had urged him never to compete in "the big leagues" of Manhattan.

" 'We don't know anything about that. Don't do it,' " Mr. Trump quoted his father as saying. "I said, 'I've got to go into Manhattan. I've got to build those big buildings. I've got to do it, Dad. I've got to do it.' "

TODD HEISLER/THE NEW YORK TIMES

Mr. Trump officially announcing his campaign for the presidency at Trump Tower on June 16, 2015.

Powered by that same grasping ambition, Mr. Trump's candidacy was marked by countless missteps and grievous errors, from the crude and meandering speeches he delivered daily, to the allegations of sexual assault that appeared to cripple him in the final weeks of the race. No other presidential candidate in memory has given offense so freely and been so battered by scandal, and lived to fight on and win.

Amid all his innumerable blunders, however, Mr. Trump got one or two things right that mattered more than all the rest. On a visceral level, he grasped dynamics that the political leadership of both parties missed or ignored — most of all, the raw frustration of blue-collar and middle-class white voters who rallied to his candidacy with decisive force.

Mr. Trump rallied them less with policy promises than with gut-level pronouncements — against foreign trade, foreign wars and foreign workers. He left his Republican primary opponents agog at his dismissals of mainstream policy, and exposed a yawning breach between the

MAX WHITTAKER FOR THE NEW YORK TIMES

Mr. Trump tossed campaign hats to the crowd aboard the battleship Iowa in Los Angeles.

program of tax cuts and fiscal austerity favored by traditional conservatives, and the preoccupations of the party's rank and file.

Ridiculed by critics on the right and left, shunned by the most respected figures in American politics, including every living former president, Mr. Trump equated his own outcast status with the resentments of the white class.

Even the invective and incivility that appalled the traditional guardians of political discourse seemed only to forge a tighter bond between Mr. Trump and his inflamed following. He dismissed American social norms as mere "political correctness," mocking the physical appearance of an opponent's wife, savaging Hillary Clinton's marriage and wielding stereotypes of racial minorities — all to the applause of his base.

In sum, Mr. Trump offered himself to the country as a tribune of white populist rage, and pledged at the Republican National Convention in Cleveland to defend "the laid-off factory workers and the communities crushed by our horrible and unfair trade deals."

"These are the forgotten men and women of our country," Mr. Trump said. "People who work hard but no longer have a voice."

He pledged: "I am your voice."

The message resonated especially in the Midwest, where a stunning victory in Ohio helped give Mr. Trump the Electoral College votes he needed to win. But his ultimate triumph was driven less by region than by race and class. His winning coalition consisted of restive whites and scarcely anyone else.

Mr. Trump's winding path to the presidency began 10 miles east of the spot where he would build Trump Tower, in the wealthy Queens enclave of Jamaica Estates, where his father's self-made real estate empire granted Mr. Trump an easy entry into the world of construction and development. He showed little interest in politics as a young man, obtaining deferments to avoid fighting in the Vietnam War but declining to participate in the protest movements of that era.

He found his way into the political arena by way of his commercial interests and social aspirations: Under the tutelage of Roy Cohn, the legendary and infamous former adviser to Senator Joseph McCarthy of Wisconsin, Mr. Trump made himself a presence at fund-raising events and political conventions. As early as the 1980s, he insinuated himself into the company of leaders in both parties, giving money to Ronald Reagan as readily as to Mario M. Cuomo, the liberal governor of New York.

But while Mr. Trump earned headlines at that stage mainly for his romantic escapades and business failures — a lurid divorce from his first wife, Ivana, and a series of corporate bankruptcies — even then he gave hints of loftier political goals. In the run-up to the 1988 presidential campaign, he traveled to New Hampshire to give a speech warning of foreign threats to American economic power.

The next year, Mr. Trump stirred fierce controversy in New York by calling loudly for the institution of the death penalty, in the aftermath of a brutal assault and rape in Central Park, though the five young men charged with the crime were later exonerated.

Still, even as he began to campaign in the early presidential primary states, blasting Mexican migrants in acid language and demanding a shutdown of Muslim immigration into the United States, Mr. Trump never entirely shed his image as a boastful but ultimately benign showman.

Republicans of august political lineage, like Jeb Bush, derided him as "an entertainer," and trusted, in the face of mounting evidence to the contrary, that voters would discard him as such in the end.

Democrats, too, who viewed Mr. Trump as plainly unelectable from the start, acknowledged at times that they might have been wrong to sneer at him early on.

Hillary Clinton, appearing on NBC's "Late Night With Seth Meyers" last winter, noted that Mr. Trump had initially provoked "hysterical laughter," before his call for a crackdown on Muslims.

"I no longer think he's funny," Mrs. Clinton said.

CHAPTER 4

President Trump's America

Donald Trump's political policies sometimes distance him from the G.O.P., and at other times place him toward the far-right conservative. As president, he has established a pattern of issuing controversial executive orders meant to follow through on campaign promises. His travel ban and immigration policies have been particularly contentious. The American public has been largely divided on Trump's decisions, and the world has yet to fully understand the circumstances of his election.

Trump's Immigration Order Expands the Definition of 'Criminal'

BY JENNIFER MEDINA | JAN. 26, 2017

AFTER PRESIDENT TRUMP signed two sweeping executive orders on immigration on Wednesday, most of the attention was on his plans to build a wall along the border with Mexico and to hold back money from "sanctuary cities." But the most immediate effect may come from language about deportation priorities that is tucked into the border wall order. It offers an expansive definition of who is considered a criminal — a category of people Mr. Trump has said he would target for deportation. Immigration agents will now have wider latitude to enforce federal laws and are being encouraged to deport broad swaths of unauthorized immigrants.

Here are some questions and answers about the changes:

Q. *Who is considered a priority for deportation?*

A. Each presidential administration must decide who it considers a priority for deportation. Mr. Trump's order focuses on anyone who has been charged with a criminal offense, even if it has not led to a conviction. He also includes, according to language in the order, anyone who has "committed acts that constitute a chargeable criminal offense," meaning anyone the authorities believe has broken any type of law — regardless of whether that person has been charged with a crime.

Mr. Trump's order also includes anyone who has engaged in "fraud or willful misrepresentation in connection with any official matter or application before a governmental agency," a category that includes anyone who has used a false Social Security number to obtain a job, as many unauthorized immigrants do. Anyone who has received a final order to leave the country, but has not left, is also considered a priority.

Finally, he allows the targeting of anyone who "in the judgment of an immigration officer" poses a risk to either public safety or national security. That gives immigration officers the broad authority they have been pressing for, and no longer requires them to receive a review from a supervisor before targeting individuals.

Q. *Who is considered a criminal?*

A. The order defines criminal loosely, and includes anyone who has crossed the border illegally — which is a criminal misdemeanor. Anyone who has abused any public benefits program is also considered a criminal under the order.

The Obama administration, which deported nearly 400,000 people per year during its first five years, initially included those convicted of minor offenses such as shoplifting. But it later changed its policy to target primarily those who had been convicted of serious crimes, were considered national security threats or were recent arrivals. By the end of President Barack Obama's time in office, around 90 percent of the country's 11 million undocumented immigrants were not considered a priority for deportation. According to the Migration Policy Institute, a nonpartisan think tank, roughly 820,000 undocumented immigrants currently have a criminal record.

Q. *Who could be affected by this?*

A. It's impossible to know how many people will be considered priorities for deportation under the new criteria. Mr. Trump's executive order could affect any unauthorized immigrant who is not protected by Deferred Action for Childhood Arrivals, which the Obama administration put in place to give young people work permits and temporary relief from deportation. (Mr. Trump has not yet made clear whether he intends to keep that program.) Immigration lawyers have already raised concerns that people with no criminal history will be swept up by the large net the administration is casting.

Q. *Can the president carry out these changes?*

A. The president has the authority to decide who should be deported. But it is unclear whether the administration will be able to — or even try to — carry out deportations as expansively as suggested in the executive order's language. First, in order to put the 15,000 additional immigration agents he wants in place around the country and along the border, Mr. Trump needs spending approval from Congress. Even then, additional detention centers would also be needed.

The most significant hurdle is the tremendous backlog in the immigration courts. Even if immigration officials initiated thousands of deportations immediately, court dates for those immigrants would be at least a year and a half away. Some immigration experts have suggested that Mr. Trump will try to push for expedited removals, which could speed the process, and give immigrants less time to find legal representation.

Q. *How does this compare with previous administrations?*

A. Mr. Trump is opening the door to deporting far more unauthorized immigrants than previous administrations. "This is the largest expansion of any president in terms of who is a priority for removal," said Steve Yale-Loehr, a professor of immigration law at Cornell University. "Every administration has to prioritize who they will go after with their limited enforcement resources. This goes further than any other president. To make it simple: If someone is here illegally they are targets for removal."

Trump Bars Refugees and Citizens of 7 Muslim Countries

BY MICHAEL D. SHEAR AND HELENE COOPER | JAN. 27, 2017

WASHINGTON — President Trump on Friday closed the nation's borders to refugees from around the world, ordering that families fleeing the slaughter in Syria be indefinitely blocked from entering the United States, and temporarily suspending immigration from several predominantly Muslim countries.

In an executive order that he said was part of an extreme vetting plan to keep out "radical Islamic terrorists," Mr. Trump also established a religious test for refugees from Muslim nations: He ordered that Christians and others from minority religions be granted priority over Muslims.

"We don't want them here," Mr. Trump said of Islamist terrorists during a signing ceremony at the Pentagon. "We want to ensure that we are not admitting into our country the very threats our soldiers are fighting overseas. We only want to admit those into our country who will support our country, and love deeply our people."

Earlier in the day, Mr. Trump explained to an interviewer for the Christian Broadcasting Network that Christians in Syria were "horribly treated" and alleged that under previous administrations, "if you were a Muslim you could come in, but if you were a Christian, it was almost impossible."

"I thought it was very, very unfair. So we are going to help them," the president said.

In fact, the United States accepts tens of thousands of Christian refugees. According to the Pew Research Center, almost as many Christian refugees (37,521) were admitted as Muslim refugees (38,901) in the 2016 fiscal year.

The executive order suspends the entry of refugees into the United States for 120 days and directs officials to determine additional screening "to ensure that those approved for refugee admission do not pose a threat to the security and welfare of the United States."

The order also stops the admission of refugees from Syria indefinitely, and bars entry into the United States for 90 days from seven predominantly Muslim countries linked to concerns about terrorism. Those countries are Iraq, Syria, Iran, Sudan, Libya, Somalia and Yemen.

Additionally, Mr. Trump signed a memorandum on Friday directing what he called "a great rebuilding of the armed services," saying it would call for budget negotiations to acquire new planes, new ships and new resources for the nation's military.

"Our military strength will be questioned by no one, but neither will our dedication to peace," Mr. Trump said.

Announcing his "extreme vetting" plan, the president invoked the specter of the Sept. 11, 2001, attacks. Most of the 19 hijackers on the planes that crashed into the World Trade Center, the Pentagon and a field in Shanksville, Pa., were from Saudi Arabia. The rest were from the United Arab Emirates, Egypt and Lebanon. None of those countries are on Mr. Trump's visa ban list.

Human rights activists roundly condemned Mr. Trump's actions, describing them as officially sanctioned religious persecution dressed up to look like an effort to make the United States safer.

The International Rescue Committee called it "harmful and hasty." The American Civil Liberties Union described it as a "euphemism for discriminating against Muslims." Raymond Offensheiser, the president of Oxfam America, said the order would harm families around the world who are threatened by authoritarian governments.

"The refugees impacted by today's decision are among the world's most vulnerable people — women, children, and men — who are simply trying to find a safe place to live after fleeing unfathomable violence and loss," Mr. Offensheiser said.

The president signed the executive order shortly after issuing a statement noting that Friday was International Holocaust

Remembrance Day, an irony that many of his critics highlighted on Twitter. The statement did not mention Jews, although it cited the "depravity and horror inflicted on innocent people by Nazi terror."

Mr. Trump's actions came during a swearing-in ceremony for Secretary of Defense Jim Mattis, a former Marine general. Standing in the Hall of Heroes at the Pentagon, Mr. Trump hailed the members of America's military as "the backbone of this country" and described Mr. Mattis as a "man of action." The president mistakenly referred to Mr. Mattis as a "soldier," a term abhorred by Marines.

Mr. Trump has been deferential to Mr. Mattis, who has quickly established himself as a top aide whose advice the president is willing to take. On Friday, Mr. Trump said he would let Mr. Mattis "override" him by banning torture during terror interrogations even though Mr. Trump believes the tactics do work in getting information from suspects.

In a remarkable show of deference to his own subordinate, Mr. Trump said during an earlier news conference Friday morning with Theresa May, the British prime minister, that he would let Mr. Mattis decide about whether to use torture in interrogations. Mr. Mattis has said he does not believe torture is effective.

"I don't necessarily agree, but I will tell you that he will override because I'm giving him that power," Mr. Trump said. "I'm going to rely on him. I happen to feel that it does work."

Mr. Trump appeared to be struggling with the issue even as he spoke, returning several times to his own belief in the effectiveness of torture even as he stated that he would let Mr. Mattis decide.

"But I'm going with our leaders," he said. "We are going to win, with or without."

Then he added, "But I do disagree."

Mr. Mattis spent his first week as defense secretary trying to reassure not only American allies, but also military rank and file, that the United States will not abandon a national security structure that has stood in place since the end of World War II. He has told officials in the Pentagon building that at an uncertain time, he intends, as defense secretary, to provide an even-keeled, measured approach to national security issues.

Before the signing ceremony, Mr. Trump met with Mr. Mattis and his military chiefs for about an hour. The meeting — which took place in a Pentagon secure room known as "the tank" — included introductions for Mr. Trump to his military chiefs of staff. The meeting was attended by Michael Flynn, the national security adviser; Gen. Joseph Dunford, chairman of the Joint Chiefs of Staff; and the chiefs of the four services and the National Guard.

The men discussed how to accelerate the fight against the Islamic State and North Korea and how to deal with a host of global challenges, said a defense official who was not authorized to talk publicly about the internal talks. The leaders also discussed how to improve military readiness.

The newly sworn-in secretary of defense also gave Mr. Trump a little of what the president has been asking — or tweeting — for. On Thursday, Mr. Mattis ordered a review of the controversial F-35 Joint Strike Fighter program, which has been criticized by Mr. Trump for its cost overruns.

Mr. Mattis also ordered that plans for a new Air Force One — another project that has come under fire from Mr. Trump — should be reviewed, "with the specific objective of identifying means to substantially reduce the program's costs while delivering needed capabilities."

The F-35 review, Mr. Mattis said in a memo, will also look at how to reduce costs while still meeting requirements set out for the fighter jet program.

During his confirmation hearings this month, Mr. Mattis defended Twitter messages from Mr. Trump criticizing the F-35 program. Mr. Mattis said at the time that Mr. Trump had "in no way shown a lack of support for the program," adding, "He just wants more bang for the buck."

The cost of building the F-35 next-generation fighter jet has been an issue at the Pentagon for several years. At an estimated $400 billion over 15 years for 2,443 planes, the fighter jet is the military's largest weapons project.

Trump Is Criticized for Not Calling Out White Supremacists

BY GLENN THRUSH AND MAGGIE HABERMAN | AUG. 12, 2017

BRIDGEWATER, N.J. — President Trump is rarely reluctant to express his opinion, but he is often seized by caution when addressing the violence and vitriol of white nationalists, neo-Nazis and alt-right activists, some of whom are his supporters.

After days of genially bombastic interactions with the news media on North Korea and the shortcomings of congressional Republicans, Mr. Trump on Saturday condemned the bloody protests in Charlottesville, Va., in what critics in both parties saw as muted, equivocal terms.

During a brief and uncomfortable address to reporters at his golf resort in Bedminster, N.J., he called for an end to the violence. But he was the only national political figure to spread blame for the "hatred, bigotry and violence" that resulted in the death of one person to "many sides."

For the most part, Republican leaders and other allies have kept quiet over several months about Mr. Trump's outbursts and angry Twitter posts. But recently they have stopped averting their gazes and on Saturday a handful criticized his reaction to Charlottesville as insufficient.

"Mr. President — we must call evil by its name," tweeted Senator Cory Gardner, Republican from Colorado, who oversees the National Republican Senatorial Committee, the campaign arm of the Senate Republicans.

"These were white supremacists and this was domestic terrorism," he added, a description several of his colleagues used.

Mike Huckabee, the former Arkansas governor and the father of the White House press secretary, Sarah Huckabee Sanders, did not dispute Mr. Trump's comments directly, but he called the behavior of white nationalists in Charlottesville "evil."

Democrats have suggested that Mr. Trump is simply unwilling to alienate the segment of his white electoral base that embraces bigotry. The president has forcefully rejected any suggestion he harbors any racial or ethnic animosities, and points to his son-in-law, Jared Kushner, an observant Jew, and his daughter Ivanka, who converted to the faith, as proof of his inclusiveness.

In one Twitter post on Saturday, Mr. Trump nodded to that inclusiveness.

"We must remember this truth: No matter our color, creed, religion or political party, we are ALL AMERICANS FIRST," the president wrote, a statement that had echoes of his campaign slogan, America First.

But like several other statements Mr. Trump made on Saturday, the tweet made no mention that the violence in Charlottesville was initiated by white supremacists brandishing anti-Semitic placards, Confederate battle flags, torches and a few Trump campaign signs.

Mr. Trump, the product of a well-to-do, predominantly white Queens enclave who in 1989 paid for a full-page ad in The New York Times calling for the death penalty for five black teenagers convicted but later exonerated of raping a white woman in Central Park, flirted with racial controversy during the 2016 campaign. He repeatedly expressed outrage that anyone could suggest he was prejudiced.

When he retweeted white supremacists' accounts, he brushed aside questions about them. When he was asked about the support he had been given by David Duke, a former Ku Klux Klan leader, he chafed, insisting he didn't know Mr. Duke.

Finally, at a news conference in South Carolina, Mr. Trump said "I disavow" when pressed on Mr. Duke. He later described Mr. Duke as a "bad person."

When his social media director, Dan Scavino, posted an image on Mr. Trump's Twitter feed with a Star of David near Hillary Clinton's head, with money raining down, Mr. Trump rejected widespread criticism of the image as anti-Semitic. And after years of questioning President Barack Obama's citizenship, he blamed others for raising the issue in the first place.

In an interview that aired in September 2016, Mr. Trump said "I am the least racist person that you have ever met," a statement he repeated at a White House news conference in February.

In Bedminster on Saturday, Mr. Trump said he and his team were "closely following the terrible events unfolding in Charlottesville, Va.," then tried to portray the violence there as a chronic, bipartisan plague. "It's been going on for a long time in our country," he said. "It's not Donald Trump, it's not Barack Obama."

Mr. Trump did not single out the marchers, who included the white supremacist Richard Spencer and Mr. Duke, for their ideology.

While Democrats and some Republicans faulted Mr. Trump for being too vague, Mr. Duke was among the few Trump critics who thought the president had gone too far.

"I would recommend you take a good look in the mirror & remember it was White Americans who put you in the presidency, not radical leftists," he wrote on Twitter, shortly after the president spoke.

The Department of Justice announced late Saturday that it was opening a civil-rights investigation into "the circumstances of the deadly vehicular incident," to be conducted by the F.B.I., the United States attorney for the Western District of Virginia, and the department's Civil Rights Division.

"The violence and deaths in Charlottesville strike at the heart of American law and justice," Attorney General Jeff Sessions said in a statement. "When such actions arise from racial bigotry and hatred, they betray our core values and cannot be tolerated."

The president remained silent on the violence for most of the morning even as House Speaker Paul D. Ryan, Mr. Trump's wife, Melania, and dozens of other public figures condemned the march.

Mrs. Trump, using her official Twitter account, wrote, "Our country encourages freedom of speech, but let's communicate w/o hate in our hearts. No good comes from violence. #Charlottesville."

Mr. Ryan was even more explicit. "The views fueling the spectacle in Charlottesville are repugnant. Let it only serve to unite Americans against this kind of vile bigotry," he wrote on Twitter at noon, around the time that Gov. Terry McAuliffe declared a state of emergency in the city.

Trump Sexual Misconduct Accusations Repeated by Several Women

BY MICHAEL D. SHEAR | DEC. 11, 2017

WASHINGTON — Several women who came forward during the 2016 campaign to accuse Donald J. Trump of sexual misconduct renewed their allegations publicly on Monday, betting that recently aggressive attitudes against harassment will give their stories new life and demanding that Congress investigate the president's actions.

The women said that they were frustrated that their stories about what they described as Mr. Trump's actions did not have a greater effect on his campaign. But they also expressed hope that they would be taken more seriously after a torrent of similar accusations had toppled the careers of powerful men in the news media, business and politics.

"Now it's just like, 'All right let's try Round 2, the environment is different, let's try again,' " Samantha Holvey, a former contestant in the Miss USA pageant, said Monday morning on the NBC program "Megyn Kelly Today." She repeated her charge that Mr. Trump ogled her and other women in the pageant's hair and makeup room.

Ms. Holvey was joined by Jessica Leeds, who has said Mr. Trump groped and kissed her during a flight in the 1970s, and Rachel Crooks, who has accused Mr. Trump of repeatedly kissing her outside her office in Trump Tower. Lisa Boyne, a fourth accuser, joined the women at a news conference hosted by Brave New Films, a documentary film company.

"After the meal was cleared, all of a sudden, he was all over me, kissing and groping and groping and kissing," Ms. Leeds said. "My memory of it was, nothing was said. He didn't say, 'Oh, by the way,' and I didn't go, 'Eek' or 'Help' or whatever; it was just this silent groping going on."

The effort by the women to attract new attention to the allegations comes amid rapidly shifting attitudes in American society about the need to hold men accountable for their treatment of women, even for acts perpetrated long ago. Several high-profile television anchors have been fired from their jobs after being accused of inappropriate touching, exposing themselves or assaulting women in the workplace.

Allegations of sexual assault against Roy S. Moore, the Republican candidate for Senate in Alabama, have roiled the special election in that state, where voting is to take place on Tuesday. Mr. Trump's decision to endorse Mr. Moore despite accusations that the Senate candidate once fondled a 14-year-old girl, has highlighted the president's own accusations.

On Monday, Senator Kirsten Gillibrand, Democrat of New York, added her name to a short list of Democratic lawmakers who have called on Mr. Trump to resign because of the sexual misconduct accusations lodged against him.

"President Trump has committed assault, according to these women," Ms. Gillibrand said Monday afternoon on CNN. "And those are very credible allegations of misconduct and criminal activity, and he should be fully investigated and he should resign." She echoed the comments of the women, saying that Congress should investigate.

Whether the president will hold himself accountable "is something you really can't hold your breath for, so Congress should have hearings," Ms. Gillibrand said.

This month, Senator Jeff Merkley, Democrat of Oregon, called on the president to step down because of a track record of "horrific conduct" with women. Senator Bernie Sanders, an independent from Vermont, said on Sunday that the president "has been accused by many women of assault" and urged him to consider resigning the way that Senator Al Franken, Democrat of Minnesota, agreed to do after multiple allegations of inappropriate behavior. Senator Cory Booker, Democrat of New Jersey, told Vice News on Sunday that the accusations by the women against Mr. Trump were "far more damning."

White House officials on Monday repeated the president's claim that the accusations of sexual misconduct were false and that the women were lying.

"The president has directly responded and said that these allegations are false and that's what I'm doing in relaying that information to you," Sarah Huckabee Sanders, the White House press secretary, told reporters. Asked whether Congress should investigate, Ms. Sanders noted that voters had already made a judgment about the allegations.

"This took place long before he was elected to be president," Ms. Sanders said. "And the people of this country, at a decisive election, supported President Trump, and we feel like these allegations have been answered through that process."

The women accusing the president originally came forward, along with several others, in October 2016 after reports emerged of Mr. Trump talking crudely on an "Access Hollywood" recording. Mr. Trump admitted to making the comments on the tape, and apologized for them, but he vehemently denied the allegations of misconduct and harassment by the other women.

After Mr. Trump's victory on Election Day, interest waned in the allegations. Several of the women said on Monday that they were angry that their decision to tell their stories did not initially seem to be taken seriously.

"It was heartbreaking last year," Ms. Holvey said on the NBC program. "We are private citizens and for us to put ourselves out there, to try to show America who this man is, and especially how he views women, for them to say, 'Meh, we don't care,' it hurt."

It remains to be seen whether the women will now be treated differently. Nikki R. Haley, the ambassador to the United Nations and a prominent woman in Mr. Trump's cabinet, broke with White House talking points on Sunday when she said that the president's accusers "should be heard" and should feel free to come forward — even though the election was over.

"I know that he was elected," Ms. Haley said on CBS's "Face the Nation." "But, you know, women should always feel comfortable coming forward. And we should all be willing to listen to them."

At the White House, Ms. Sanders responded to a question about Ms. Haley's comments by saying that the president agreed — in generic terms — that "it's a good thing that women are coming forward" to tell their stories about harassment.

But she said that "he also feels strongly that a mere allegation shouldn't determine the course," and she repeated Mr. Trump's belief that his victory in the election should be the end of the story.

"The American people knew this and voted for the president," Ms. Sanders said. "And we feel like we're ready to move forward in that process."

It's Trump's Economy Now

OPINION | BY STEPHEN MOORE | JAN. 28, 2018

IF YOU CAN, put aside for a moment your opinion of Donald Trump's words and actions and let's be perfectly honest: One year into his presidency, could the economy be any rosier?

The economy grew at a rate of about 3 percent in the last three quarters, something that economists said was very unlikely just a year ago. The more than 40 percent increase in the Dow Jones industrial average since Election Day means a nearly $7 trillion jump in wealth. That has benefited the rich, yes, but every one of the 55 million Americans with a 401(k) plan, the 20 million with IRAs and the millions more with public and private pension plans have benefited, too. I would argue that investors are turning lower business tax rates on profits and the administration's rollback of regulations into higher stock valuations.

The job market improved impressively under Barack Obama's presidency after the Great Recession, when millions of jobs vanished seemingly overnight. But the past year's continued decline in joblessness is impressive as well. In recent weeks, the number of new unemployment insurance claims and the unemployment rate for blacks and Hispanics have been at or near their lowest levels in more than four decades.

Then there is the cheerful news for the Rust Belt areas of the country: Blue-collar manufacturing, construction and mining jobs have risen by almost half a million in just one year.

All of this is punctuated by the daily news of more jobs, higher pay and fresh investment in America just one month into the Trump tax cut. Apple's plan to bring some $250 billion in profits back to America, create 20,000 jobs, open a new business campus and pay $38 billion in taxes to the Treasury Department is just the kind of response we hoped for from lowering corporate and repatriation taxes.

Fiat Chrysler has announced it is moving an auto factory to Michigan with 2,500 jobs. After decades of outsourcing jobs from America, companies are creating jobs here. In recent days, we have seen similar announcements of worker bonuses or new hiring from Disney, Home Depot, JPMorgan Chase, FedEx and other companies.

A new Quinnipiac poll finds that two-thirds of American voters now rate the economy as good or great, the highest number since the question was first asked 17 years ago.

Admittedly, these are short-term trends, based on just one year of Mr. Trump's term. If I've learned anything as an economic analyst, it is that the stock market and economic winds can shift by the hour. But for now, it's hard to see many dark clouds on the horizon. They will come, of course, as they do for almost every president. But few presidents can claim to have presided over the kind of economy the United States is enjoying now. And surely the primal screams from both the right and left that President Trump would ruin the economy now seem hysterical.

So who gets the credit for this surge? Most voters say President Obama — and, sure, he gets some because corporate balance sheets were healthy when Mr. Trump entered office. But there are several holes in this theory. For one, the economy was decelerating at the end of the Obama presidency, with the annual growth rate falling to an anemic 1.6 percent in 2016, and many economists warned of a recession.

If Mr. Trump had continued Mr. Obama's policies, one might not credit him for today's strong economy. But Mr. Trump has begun to systematically overturn Obama policies on taxes, regulations, energy, climate change, net neutrality, budget priorities and health care — as well as replacing Janet Yellen as chairwoman of the Federal Reserve. Trumponomics is Obamanomics in reverse.

In the first 18 months of the Reagan presidency, the economy plummeted and the president's liberal critics triumphantly declared Reaganomics a failure. But by late 1982, with Reagan's phased-in tax cuts finally kicking in, the economy exploded and quarterly growth rates hit 8 percent, job creation soared and Reagan won re-election in a 49-state landslide.

If the economy had nose-dived in 2017, there's no doubt the media would have pounced on Trump policies as disgraceful failures. But with the economy red-hot, he gets little credit. That's a double standard.

Ultimately, the most important statistical indicator for Mr. Trump will be wages for middle-income workers. They've been flat in real terms for 15 years, which more than anything explains the populist rebellion in 2016. So far, wages and salaries haven't bumped up much, but we are betting that the tax cut will bring increased investment and a supertight job market with intense competition for workers leading to higher pay. This is already starting to happen at Walmart and other companies, and in fast-growing cities like Nashville and San Francisco.

If those wages go up, Mr. Trump may not get credit from the news media or Democrats, but it's a good bet he will get re-elected.

STEPHEN MOORE, A SENIOR FELLOW AT THE HERITAGE FOUNDATION, WAS A SENIOR ECONOMIC ADVISER TO THE TRUMP CAMPAIGN.

Once Again, Push for Gun Control Collides With Political Reality

BY CARL HULSE | FEB. 28, 2018

WASHINGTON — Here's how significant things don't get done in Washington even in a moment of crisis and opportunity.

The president throws out a hodgepodge of ideas, thoroughly confusing both sides about what he really supports. Senate Republicans, grappling for an answer that responds to public clamor but doesn't alienate their conservative base, would prefer instead to focus on a small fix unlikely to satisfy many people even if it could overcome internal divisions. House Republicans say they will wait to see what the Senate does — though history has shown that can be a very long wait. Democrats push for a broad debate that Republicans want nothing to do with.

That's where Washington stands now on the subject of new gun legislation after the school shooting in Parkland, Fla. Despite immense public pressure in part from students who escaped the attack, the outlook for any consequential action remains dim as the president and lawmakers diverge on how best to respond.

President Trump upended the discussion on Wednesday during a bipartisan White House meeting with lawmakers. He seemed to side more with Democrats than Republicans on gun rights, chided fellow Republicans for fearing the National Rifle Association and even suggested that guns should be summarily confiscated from suspects who raise red flags, forcing them to go to court to regain them. Such an approach toward gun rights runs counter to Republican dogma, as did other suggestions that the president made.

But the meeting was very similar to an earlier White House session in which the president seemed to join with Democrats on divisive immigration policy only to later reverse course, leaving the parties at an impasse. Members of both parties expressed skepticism on Wednesday that the White House meeting would lead to a breakthrough. They even suggested that it could prove counterproductive by forcing the gun lobby to dig in its heels and by making Republican leaders unwilling to push ahead given the possibility of glaring divisions with Mr. Trump. Officials said the next issue on the Senate agenda was likely to be a rollback of banking regulations, not increased gun control.

Mr. Trump's stream-of-consciousness display was just the latest wrinkle in the contentious struggle over gun safety. The most widely backed response to the Parkland shooting would provide new incentives for public agencies to submit information that could disqualify prospective gun buyers to the National Instant Criminal Background Check System, an action most agree is modest at best.

Even though they support it themselves, leading Democrats consider that proposal, sponsored by Senator John Cornyn of Texas, the No. 2 Republican, to be woefully insufficient given the scope of the mass shootings.

"The Cornyn bill is kind of a fig leaf," said Senator Claire McCaskill of Missouri, one of the Democrats up for re-election in a state that President Trump carried in 2016.

To Democrats, the fact that the N.R.A. is not opposed to the proposal is prima facie evidence that it falls short. They are demanding a more robust debate over a series of gun initiatives, notably what they call a "universal" background check system that would cover all gun transactions in the country. That plan is opposed by the gun lobby but was seemingly endorsed by Mr. Trump, putting him at odds not only with the gun advocacy group that strongly backed him, but with many congressional Republicans, as well.

Senator Christopher S. Murphy, Democrat of Connecticut and an author, with Mr. Cornyn, of the more limited background check bill, equated taking up his own legislation without allowing consideration of alternatives to "slamming the door in the face of all these kids who are demanding change."

"I think it is imperative that we rise to the moment," Mr. Murphy said.

Mr. Trump told lawmakers they should use a broader bipartisan background check measure that failed in 2013 after the school shooting in Newtown, Conn., as the basis for a comprehensive measure that could take in many proposals, including the Cornyn plan, new mental health provisions and added security for schools. He urged backers of a renewed ban on assault weapons to make their case to the authors of the legislation and said he would welcome the opportunity to enact one sweeping bill to combat mass shootings. But Congress has for years been unable to make even incremental headway on new gun buying limits, let alone the type of multifaceted plan called for by the president.

Democrats would like to persuade Senator Mitch McConnell, Republican of Kentucky and the majority leader, to allow votes on major gun control proposals, a plan that could throw the Senate into a full-blown showdown over competing initiatives. But Mr. McConnell is never one to rush into a fight that divides his own party if he can help it. While Mr. McConnell has been quiet about his intentions, Mr. Cornyn opened the door to that possibility of a wider debate provided it could get to passage of his bill at a minimum.

"We can set up a situation where they can vote on those amendments," he said. "What I don't want to do is leave here this week and go back home to Texas and say we failed to do anything to try to address these tragedies."

As lawmakers quibbled about how to proceed, some of the multiple proposals promoted by Mr. Trump were falling by the wayside.

Republican lawmakers seem uninterested in plans to raise the age to buy all guns to 21. The idea of arming teachers was also getting a cold reception. Among plans circulating that could draw bipartisan support was a measure that would prevent those on federal no-fly lists from buying guns, though that approach has met Republican resistance in the past.

Hoping to skirt a divisive debate, Republicans preferred to focus on other remedies, like improving general school safety, while pointing to law enforcement failures surrounding the Parkland shooting.

Democrats remained doubtful that Republicans would be willing to buck the N.R.A., particularly in an election year, but said it would be an imperative for legislative success.

“You can’t solve this problem and please the N.R.A.,” said Senator Chuck Schumer of New York, the Democratic leader. “Our Republican colleagues need to learn that.”

Given longstanding political conflict over the issue, many lawmakers in both parties anticipate the push for new laws will likely fall apart as so many others have in the aftermath of mass shootings.

If that is the outcome, the determined high school students and their allies who have helped drive the debate to this point seem unlikely to let the issue go. Maybe the difference this time isn’t that Congress will act, but it is that those pushing Congress will not allow lawmakers to so quickly move on after they don’t.

Suddenly, the G.O.P. Remembers All Its Doubts on Trump

BY CARL HULSE | MARCH 7, 2018

WASHINGTON — Over the past week, congressional Republicans have gotten a glimpse of the President Trump they hoped to never see.

On gun safety and, more significantly to many of them, trade, the president has loudly broken with longstanding party orthodoxy and reminded Republican leaders on Capitol Hill that they can never be 100 percent certain of what they are going to get with the onetime New York Democrat.

Despite such worries, Mr. Trump's first-year actions on policy and personnel — particularly judicial nominees — provided substantial reassurance to congressional Republicans. They concluded that Mr. Trump was really one of them when it came to bedrock issues and that the anti-Washington, drain-the-swamp cries from the raucous campaign rallies were only so many applause lines.

In the chaos of the early weeks of his administration, Mr. Trump provoked a sigh of relief from Senator Mitch McConnell, Republican of Kentucky and the majority leader, that the president seemed to actually be conservative. "If you look at the steps that have been taken so far, looks good to me," Mr. McConnell said.

Now here comes Mr. Trump with his sudden proposal to rebuild the country's steel and aluminum industries through steep tariffs on imports from leading trading partners. Most congressional Republicans fundamentally disagree with that approach, which they consider a backdoor tax that could easily touch off a calamitous trade war, hurt their local businesses and overwhelm any gains from their hard-won, Republican-only tax bill.

Already facing a harsh political climate heading toward the November midterm elections, Republicans fear that moving ahead with the tariffs could send the party — not to mention the economy — spiraling

DAMON WINTER/THE NEW YORK TIMES

Recordings of Donald J. Trump reveal a man who is fixated on his own celebrity, anxious about losing his status and contemptuous of those who fall from grace.

in the wrong direction. Republicans are banking on a robust economy that they can attribute to their tax cuts and regulatory rollbacks to overcome the deep public disapproval of Mr. Trump exhibited in multiple elections last year. They don't want to do anything that could threaten economic gains.

"The economy is moving in the right direction; that is what we are working on," Senator John Thune of South Dakota, the chamber's No. 3 Republican, told reporters on Tuesday. "We are going to stay focused on a pro-growth, pro-jobs agenda."

Mr. McConnell had remained quiet about the tariffs since Mr. Trump unexpectedly announced them last week. But on Tuesday, he made it very clear that he, and almost all of his colleagues, have major problems with them.

"There's a high level of concern about interfering with what appears to be an economy that's taking off in every respect," Mr. McConnell said. "I think the best way to characterize where I am, and where our members are, is we are urging caution that this develop into something much more dramatic that could send the economy in the wrong direction."

This major policy divide goes to a disconnect between the president and congressional Republican leaders that has been papered over by fights with Democrats over the past year as well as the party unity behind the tax bill.

Most of the Republican leaders on Capitol Hill remain firmly aligned with big business and want to retain the strong support of advocacy groups such as the U.S. Chamber of Commerce and organizations affiliated with David H. and Charles G. Koch. Those business factions, always important to Republicans in a campaign year, do not like new tariffs.

Mr. Trump, on the other hand, has for years preached about the dangers and disadvantages of free trade and the harm it has done to once-leading American industries. Republicans now hoping to talk the president down from his tariff stance may find that his campaign promises about protectionism are ones he truly wants to keep.

It is a similar situation with gun safety. Mr. Trump has in the past backed the idea of an assault weapons ban. But congressional Republicans figured that his strong campaign embrace of the National Rifle Association would keep him securely in the anti-gun-control corner.

Then, in last week's extraordinary public White House meeting after the Parkland, Fla., school massacre, Mr. Trump embraced multiple aspects of the gun control agenda. He even uttered the words "take the guns first" — a phrase previously unthinkable for a top Republican politician given the party's history on gun rights.

Republicans were aghast. They also figured that, under pressure from his allies at the N.R.A., Mr. Trump would quickly return to the fold and let his enthusiasm for gun control wane. More important, congressional Republicans also knew that gun control legislation was really in their hands, not the administration's, and that they could easily bottle up any proposal.

But tariffs are a completely different matter, with the president given wide latitude to act on international trade policy. Republicans, who say they have little legislative recourse, are now engaged in a furious effort to pull the president back from making too sweeping a decision.

They are also treading carefully to avoid antagonizing a mercurial figure whose mind they still hope to change as they have in previous cases where he drifted from the party line, such as on immigration.

Speaker Paul D. Ryan, for instance, was careful to credit Mr. Trump on Tuesday for exposing that some countries do take advantage of the trade rules.

"The president's right to point out that there are abuses," Mr. Ryan said. "There clearly is dumping and transshipping of steel and aluminum."

Referring to any trade restrictions, Mr. Ryan said that Republicans simply "want to make sure that it's done in a prudent way that's more surgical, so we can limit unintended consequences."

As for Mr. McConnell, he said that "we need to wait and see what the White House finally decides to do on this."

Mr. McConnell would no doubt prefer that Mr. Trump revert to the conventional conservative principles the senator found so comforting last year. But this break could prove to be real, putting Mr. Trump and his Republican allies at cross-purposes at an inauspicious moment on the political calendar.

Trump's Meeting With Kim Jong-un Is Another Pledge to Do What Nobody Else Can

BY PETER BAKER | MARCH 8, 2018

WASHINGTON — When the establishment told him he should talk with North Korea, President Trump scorned the idea. "Presidents and their administrations have been talking to North Korea for 25 years" and had been made to look like "fools," he scoffed, and then rattled his saber. "Sorry, but only one thing will work!"

Five months later, Mr. Trump cast aside his skepticism and agreed to talk to North Korea with no more promise of success at negotiating an end to its nuclear and missile programs than his predecessors had. The main difference this time around is who will do the talking for the United States: Donald J. Trump.

Shocking and yet somehow not surprising, Mr. Trump's decision to do what no other sitting president has done and meet in person with a North Korean leader reflects an audacious and supremely self-confident approach to international affairs. Whether it is Middle East peace or trade agreements, Mr. Trump has repeatedly claimed that he can achieve what has eluded every other occupant of his office through the force of his own personality.

So far, he has little to show for that. He has yet to successfully negotiate any new trade deals or renegotiate any old ones. A resolution between Israel and the Palestinians, which he once said would be "maybe not as difficult as people have thought," looks more distant than when he came into office. Beyond threatening "fire and fury," he has offered no original formula that suggests a path to unlock the North Korea puzzle.

But in his penchant for unpredictability, his willingness to shift at a moment's notice and his sense that only he can make the important decisions, Mr. Trump may find a kindred spirit in the man who would sit across the table, Kim Jong-un of North Korea.

"In some ways there's a symmetry," said Wendy R. Sherman, a longtime former diplomat who was part of a historic American delegation to Pyongyang under President Bill Clinton and later negotiated the Iran nuclear agreement for President Barack Obama. "You have two leaders who believe fundamentally that they are the only people who matter."

Other presidents left talks with North Korea to lower-level officials because they did not want to reward Pyongyang with the prestige of such a meeting unless there was a substantial assurance of a breakthrough. They feared an ill-conceived gathering that resulted in failure would be counterproductive.

Mr. Clinton considered going to Pyongyang in the twilight months of his presidency, but ultimately opted against it, partly because of the Florida recount that dominated the postelection period in 2000 and partly because he calculated he had a better chance of forging an agreement between Israel and the Palestinians in the time he had left. He was unable to achieve that either, but after leaving office, went to North Korea to bring home two Americans held prisoner.

Diplomacy is a positive, Ms. Sherman said. "But this is a diplomacy that has to be prepared. It's why Bill Clinton didn't drop everything and go to Pyongyang." She added: "This is very serious business. It is not a reality show. And it's our national security that is at stake."

While the president's economic pressure may have prompted him to come to the table, Mr. Kim made few known concessions to win a meeting with Mr. Trump. The North Korean leader agreed to suspend nuclear and missile tests for the moment, although after a year of accelerated tests, they may not be as necessary for the program's development at this point. And he assented to routine joint military exercises by the United States and South Korea that usually draw his ire.

"I can't imagine any other president doing this on the basis of these general comments passed on from Kim Jong-un," said Christopher R.

Hill, who negotiated with North Korea for President George W. Bush. "The question is whether Trump will go ahead without clear signs the North Koreans are on the way to denuclearization."

Among those surprised by the president's decision to meet Mr. Kim were some of his own advisers. "In terms of direct talks with the United States, you ask negotiations and we're a long ways from negotiations," Secretary of State Rex W. Tillerson told reporters traveling with him in Africa just hours before the surprise announcement at the White House.

But the president has flirted with the idea of meeting Mr. Kim before, and James Jay Carafano, a national security scholar at the Heritage Foundation, said it was utterly predictable that Mr. Trump would want to personally take on the issue.

"Trump actually has a really good track record of talking to other leaders," Mr. Carafano said. "We ought to get beyond this thing that he's going to be stupid. He's now met with dozens of world leaders. This is actually where he shines, meeting with other leaders and looking very presidential. The fact that he would want to look the guy in the eye is very Trumpian."

Indeed, Mr. Trump has been far more eager to deal directly with foreign leaders than Mr. Obama, a hands-on interlocutor who has forged relationships that changed his views and policies, such as with President Xi Jinping of China.

Mr. Carafano said Mr. Trump, the first president never to have served in government or the military, is not wedded to stale nostrums and is willing to think outside the box. He cited Mr. Trump's decision to recognize Jerusalem as Israel's capital, a move Democratic and Republican presidents were too wary to make. While it drew loud protests from Palestinians, Mr. Carafano said, the world did not come to an end.

But Mr. Carafano cautioned against expecting a breakthrough if the meeting with Mr. Kim takes place. "The odds of him actually negotiating something are incredibly small," he said. But the president's agreement to talk dispels the warnings by critics that Mr. Trump was inevitably headed to war with North Korea through his bellicose messaging. "Our policy is not on this inevitable path to World War III."

Still, the critics remain dubious. While they have urged Mr. Trump to try diplomacy, many said they did not mean that he should do it personally, and they warned that the president did not seem to have a thought-through plan for what he could reasonably achieve and how he would do it. Given Mr. Trump's repeated criticism of Mr. Obama's Iran deal — and a looming deadline for deciding whether to scrap it — the president would be hard pressed to agree to any accord with North Korea that fell short of its terms.

"Trump sees himself as a master negotiator, and yet is not particularly good at it," said Colin Kahl, a former national security official under Mr. Obama. "He isn't thoughtful or steeped in the types of details required for this type of diplomacy. He is prone to manipulation and flattery. He often makes threats he doesn't follow through on and promises he can't or won't keep. And he often throws allies under the bus. This does not add up to a recipe for success, and the stakes could not be higher."

But the president's aides said he was full of surprises and should not be discounted. While noting that this would be a meeting, not a negotiation, a senior administration official, who briefed reporters on the condition of anonymity, said Mr. Trump was elected in part because he was willing to take approaches different from those of other presidents, a trait best exemplified by his North Korea policy.

Mr. Kim is the undisputed master of his totalitarian system, the official said, and so it made sense to accept an invitation to meet with the one person who can actually make decisions instead of repeating the long slog of the past.

The real question, then, becomes whether the only two leaders who can make decisions can make one together.

When the Leader of the Free World Is an Ugly American

OPINION | BY THOMAS MEANEY AND STEPHEN WERTHEIM | MARCH 9, 2018

BAD TIMES are often interesting times. So it is with President Trump, whose insults and assaults have caused his critics to rethink what they know about their country. For the past year, American intellectuals have largely risen to the challenge, igniting new debates about race, class, gender and democracy itself. Whether these debates will translate into electoral victory remains unclear, but at least Mr. Trump's foes are grappling with the forces behind his rise. The president's critics realize that long-festering social divisions must be confronted.

But one area of debate has remained strikingly stagnant. On foreign policy, Trumpism's critics wax nostalgic for an imagined golden age before the president took office. The foreign policy establishment — from media pundits to think-tank wonks to government veterans — has reached near-perfect harmony in insisting that he radically departs from American foreign policy since World War II. The news this week that he intends to introduce tariffs on steel and aluminum is seen as just one more dramatic deviation.

These critics exaggerate Mr. Trump's abnormality, allowing him to outperform prognostications of doom. This line of thinking offers nothing better than the status quo ante that voters found uninspiring at best and repellent at worst. In effect, our finest minds are using this president to avoid addressing the problems of American foreign policy.

How did Mr. Trump manage to confound America's foreign policy mandarins? The trouble began during the campaign, when he pitted the United States against the world. On one level, this bluster promised the same thing candidates always do: Win wars decisively or don't wage them; get more benefits for fewer burdens. But after Mr. Trump chanted "America First," a string of experts concluded he'd resurrected the so-called isolationism of the 1930s, rather than believing him when he explained he was just seeking a good slogan (one not unlike John McCain's "Country First" from 2008). And what was the harm in piling on? The brute deserved to be barred from office. Branding him an isolationist seemed disqualifying.

This warning — delivered by scores of bipartisan national security experts — failed to dissuade voters. Still, the experts stuck with it. They detected isolationism in everything from his inaugural address to his withdrawal from the Trans-Pacific Partnership, which even Hillary Clinton had pledged to abandon. This misdiagnosis handed Mr. Trump the opportunity to outflank his critics. When he bombed a Syrian airfield, Jeffrey Goldberg, the editor of The Atlantic, wondered whether the president was "something wholly unique in the history of the presidency: an isolationist interventionist," as though yoking opposites together provided insight rather than revealed confusion. Mr. Trump now says he is willing to meet with Kim Jong-un of North Korea, more proof that catastrophe-mongering leaves his critics flat-footed.

Just over a year in, Mr. Trump has escalated military operations in every theater. He has endorsed NATO and doubled down on America's traditional alliances from Japan to Saudi Arabia. Few can call him an isolationist full stop.

Nevertheless, the president's critics continue to insist that he is retracting American power in some unprecedented way, rather than attempting to extend it more ruthlessly. Ben Rhodes, one of Barack Obama's chief policy advisers, casts the Trump doctrine as "America Last." Richard Haass, president of the Council on Foreign Relations, charges the president with giving up a "position of leadership in developing the rules and arrangements at the heart of any world order." Acknowledging that Mr. Trump is not retreating to isolation, the critics now advance a subtler case — that he is wrecking what they describe as the America-led "liberal international order."

Leave aside, for a moment, why Mr. Trump is said to spurn such a liberal order whereas George W. Bush, who broke international law by invading

Iraq, is having his reputation resuscitated. Leave aside that Ronald Reagan pulled out of UNESCO 34 years before Mr. Trump followed suit. Leave aside that a version of the Trump administration's steel tariff was imposed by Mr. Bush in 2002. Leave aside that Dwight Eisenhower threatened to use nuclear weapons in defense of the tiny islands of Quemoy and Matsu.

Beyond being a historical myth, is the rallying cry of the "liberal international order" likely to impress voters?

Foreign policy experts are betting on a fantasy, one mostly confined to the Acela Express. Those experts who seek to shape public opinion, to judge by their columns, interviews and tweets, have faced this responsibility only halfway. The president could not be luckier. Little short of catastrophe will vindicate his critics. Mr. Trump can clear their low bar by being unspectacularly awful. More important, the current debate does nothing to forge a future foreign policy that improves on what preceded Mr. Trump's election. Far from devising alternatives, experts are shutting down needed debate by collapsing America's interests into an abstract "order." They increasingly resemble the "globalists" whom candidate Trump derided.

The irony is, Mr. Trump was wrong. Policymakers have always put American interests first, adjusting (or defying) the rules accordingly. In 1945, Harry Truman met Winston Churchill and Josef Stalin in war-torn Potsdam, Germany. If this was the moment of creation of the "liberal international order," as today's commentators maintain, Truman did not know it. (Neither he nor his advisers used the phrase.) The frustrated president wrote to his wife, Bess, "I have to make it perfectly plain to them at least once a day that so far as this President is concerned Santa Claus is dead and that my first interest is U.S.A."

Truman understood what Mr. Trump's critics implicitly deny: the possibility that American power can come at the expense of others. The foreign policy establishment clings to the fiction that what's good for America is necessarily good for the world. They condemn Mr. Trump's tariffs as an unthinkable breach even though the United States has employed protectionist measures throughout history. They pretend that Mr. Trump, having vowed to take things from the world, must be diminishing American power when he seeks to expand it. Mr. Trump's actions may not have their intended effect, but the most logical and cutting response isn't that he is weakening America but that he's trying to strengthen it in a way we should not want. His outpouring of militarism and chauvinism may or may not reduce the United States' influence. It does, however, threaten to turn the world's sole superpower into an unabashed purveyor of violence and exploitation.

Let's call Mr. Trump's vision what it is: radical American imperialism. He does not so much break with tradition as bring forward some of its most retrograde but persistent elements. Recognizing this is the start of an honest conversation about the Trump administration and America's role in a changing world. So far, however, the right has come closer to grasping this point than the left or the center. Mr. Trump and his supporters do identify a conflict (indeed, almost endless conflict) between America's interests and the world's. As Rush Limbaugh recently put it, Mr. Trump wants to restore the "primacy of the United States," whereas his critics think "American leadership should preside over the weakening of America." The point is perverse, but it is coherent. Fearing decline, the Trumpian right seeks to get tough with the world and take all it can.

Mr. Trump's challenge can be met. As distributional conflicts surge in domestic politics, they are surging in foreign policy, too — and those who ignore them lose out to those who inflate them. Citizens seeking a better foreign policy ought to be engaged, not ignored. But recent events cast doubt on whether our current crop of experts is up to the job.

Democracy requires experts but it also requires something from them: that they facilitate public debate and respect the ultimate power of the electorate to set the aims of the nation. By rallying behind the lowest common denominator of "anything but Trump," they are disengaging the public's discontent, pulling up the drawbridge until the next election. In that sense, Donald Trump is not the only one who might be called an isolationist.

STEPHEN WERTHEIM (@STEPHENWERTHEIM) IS A LECTURER IN HISTORY AT BIRKBECK, UNIVERSITY OF LONDON. **THOMAS MEANEY** IS A FELLOW AT THE AMERICAN COUNCIL ON GERMANY.

6 Highlights From Trump's News Conference

BY THE NEW YORK TIMES | JUNE 12, 2018

PRESIDENT TRUMP held a news conference in Singapore on Tuesday after his meeting with the North Korean leader, Kim Jong-un. Below are excerpts from his remarks.

WILL KIM JONG-UN RETURN REMAINS AND DESTROY A NUCLEAR SITE?

I think he'll do it. I really believe that, otherwise I wouldn't be doing this. I really believe, and — it was really the engine-testing site, in addition to all of the other things that they've agreed to do. It was the — they have a very powerful engine-testing site, that again we're able to see because of the heat that it emits. And, yeah, I'm able to — I'm very happy, I'll tell you what, I'm very happy with those two points, the two points you mentioned, but I think you might be referring to the thing that's not in, which is the engine-testing site.

Honestly, I think he's going to do these things. I may be wrong, I mean I may stand before you in six months and say, hey, I was wrong — I don't know that I'll ever admit that, but I'll find some kind of an excuse.

THE VIDEO OF THE NORTH'S FUTURE, WITH BEACHES AND CONDOS

I told him, "You may not want this. You may want to do a much smaller version of this. I mean, you're going to do something, but you may want to do a smaller version. You may not want that, with trains, super everything at the top. And maybe you won't want that."

It's going to be up to them. It's going to be up to the people, what they want. And they may not want that, and I understand that too. It's a version of what could happen, what could take place As an example. they have great beaches. You see that whenever they're exploding their cannons into the ocean, right? I said "Boy, look at that view. Wouldn't that make a great condo?" And I explained, I said, instead of doing that you could have the best hotels in the world right there. Think of it from a real estate perspective. You have South Korea, you have China and they own the land in the middle. How bad is that, right? It's great.

HONORING AN AMERICAN WHO DIED AFTER BEING DETAINED IN NORTH KOREA

Otto Warmbier is a very special person, and he will be for a long time in my life. His parents are good friends of mine. I think without Otto, this would not have happened. Something happened from that day — it was a terrible thing, it was brutal, but a lot of people started to focus on what was going on, including North Korea. I really think that Otto is someone who did not die in vain. I told this to his parents. Special young man, and I have to say special parents, special people. Otto did not die in vain. He had a lot to do with us being here today.

THE U.S. MILITARY PRESENCE IN SOUTH KOREA

I have to be honest, and I used to say this during my campaign, as you know probably better than most — I want to get our soldiers out. I want to bring our soldiers back home. We have right now 32,000 soldiers in South Korea, and I'd like to be able to bring them back home. But that's not part of the equation right now. At some point I hope it will be, but not right now.

We will be stopping the war games, which will save us a tremendous amount of money, unless and until we see the future negotiation is not going along like it should. But we'll be saving a tremendous amount of money, plus I think it's very provocative.

ON THE G-7 PHOTO THAT DREW ATTENTION ONLINE

We finished the meeting, really, everybody was happy and I asked for changes, I demanded changes and those changes were made. In fact, the picture with Angela Merkel, who I get along with very well, where I'm sitting there like this. That picture was, we're waiting for the document, because I want to see the final document as changed by the changes that I requested.

Those were very friendly — I know it didn't look friendly and I know it was being reported sort of nasty both ways. I was angry at her or she — actually, we were just talking, the whole group, about something unrelated to everything, very friendly, waiting for the document to come back so that I could read it before I leave. Anyway.

I left and it was very friendly. When I got onto the plane, I think that Justin probably didn't know that Air Force One has about 20 televisions, and I see the television and he's giving a news conference about how he will not be pushed around by the United States.

And I say, "push him around"? We just shook hands. It was very friendly.

ON CALLING KIM "VERY TALENTED"

He is very talented. Anybody that takes over a situation like he did at 26 years of age, and is able to run it and run it tough, I don't say it was nice or I don't say anything about it, he ran it — very few people at that age, you can take one out of 10,000 probably couldn't do it.

How Trump Has Split With His Administration on Russian Meddling

BY LINDA QIU | MARCH 16, 2018

WASHINGTON — President Trump has long avoided blaming — or even naming — Russia for meddling in the 2016 election that put him in office.

But his administration has been far tougher on Moscow for cyberattacks that officials this week said not only sought to sway political opinions, but also wormed into power plants, aviation systems and other critical infrastructure in the United States and Europe.

On Thursday, Mr. Trump was studiously silent as his administration imposed sanctions on Russia for interfering in the 2016 presidential campaign and what officials called other "malicious cyberattacks." (The president did agree with a British assessment that Moscow was

TOM BRENNER/THE NEW YORK TIMES

President Trump was studiously silent as his administration imposed sanctions on Russia for interfering in the 2016 presidential campaign and what officials called other "malicious cyberattacks."

responsible for a nerve-gas attack in England against a former Russian spy and his daughter.)

The Treasury Department said the sanctions were to punish "Russia's continuing destabilizing activities." And for the first time, the Department of Homeland Security and the F.B.I. directly accused Russia of committing cyberattacks against "energy, nuclear, commercial facilities, water, aviation and critical manufacturing sectors."

Last week, by contrast, Mr. Trump said that "the Russians had no impact on our votes whatsoever."

"But, certainly, there was meddling and probably there was meddling from other countries and maybe other individuals," the president said at a March 6 news conference.

This pattern of diversion has steadily increased since Mr. Trump took office. Here is a look back at how the president and his own administration have parted ways on Russia.

February 2018: Deflecting accusations of Russian meddling. United States intelligence officials warned in mid-February that Russia had already begun meddling in the 2018 midterm elections. But Mr. Trump continued to suggest other countries could also be the culprit.

"By the way, I have to say, Obama was the president during all of this meddling, or whatever you want to call it, with Russians and others possibly," he said in a Feb. 24 interview on Fox News.

December 2017: Conflicting signals on national security. Mr. Trump's first national security strategy blueprint made repeated references to Russia's interference in the 2016 election and its "information operations as part of its offensive cyberefforts to influence public opinion across the globe."

Yet in his speech announcing the strategy on Dec. 18, Mr. Trump made one fleeting mention of Russia: of how it and China "seek to challenge American influence, values and wealth." He made no mention of Russian meddling and instead praised intelligence sharing between Russia and the United States in the face of terrorism threats.

August 2017: Signing a sanctions bill reluctantly. After Congress passed legislation in late July to impose sanctions on Russia and limit the president's authority to lift them, Mr. Trump signed the bill but criticized it as "seriously flawed — particularly because it encroaches on the executive branch's authority to negotiate."

Mr. Trump signed the legislation on Aug. 2. Several days earlier, President Vladimir V. Putin's government had retaliated by seizing two American diplomatic compounds in Russia and telling the United States Embassy in Moscow to reduce its staff across the country. Mr. Trump did not respond, and Sarah Huckabee Sanders, the White House press secretary, declined to comment.

However, the State Department described Moscow's move as "a regrettable and uncalled-for act."

"We are assessing the impact of such a limitation and how we will respond to it," the department said in a statement.

July 2017: Suggesting he found Mr. Putin's denial persuasive. After Mr. Trump met with Mr. Putin during a Group of 20 summit meeting, he recounted the Russian leader's assurances that Moscow did not intervene in the 2016 election.

"First question — first 20, 25 minutes — I said, 'Did you do it?' He said, 'No, I did not, absolutely not.' I then asked him a second time, in a totally different way. He said, 'Absolutely not,' " Mr. Trump said in an interview with Reuters that was published on July 12. "Somebody did say if he did do it, you wouldn't have found out about it. Which is a very interesting point."

January 2017: Playing down Russian cyberattacks. On Jan. 6, the intelligence community released a declassified report of its conclusions about a Russian cyberattack on the election. In a statement about his briefing on the cyberattacks that day, Mr. Trump pointed to "Russia, China, other countries."

Days before his inauguration, at a Jan. 11 news conference where he was asked whether he believed Mr. Putin ordered the hacking of American political committees, Mr. Trump said that "as far as hacking, I think it was Russia."

He then added, "But I think we also get hacked by other countries and other people."

Mr. Trump's dismissiveness of accusations of Russian interference predates his time in the White House.

Late December 2016: Praising Putin in the wake of sanctions. On Dec. 29, President Barack Obama issued sanctions against Russia and ejected 35 suspected Russian intelligence operators from the United States as punishment for Moscow's attempts to influence the election. But in a move widely believed to be aimed at fostering good relations with the incoming Trump administration, Mr. Putin announced on Dec. 30 that he would not retaliate.

Mr. Trump promptly praised Mr. Putin's decision.

A day later, Mr. Trump said he still wasn't convinced that Russia had interfered in the election, telling reporters: "And I know a lot about hacking. And hacking is a very hard thing to prove. So it could be somebody else."

Early December 2016: Disparaging intelligence agencies after reports on Russian interference. After reports in December by the The New York Times and The Washington Post that United States intelligence assessments had concluded that Russian election meddling sought to aid Mr. Trump, the president-elect disagreed.

In an unsigned statement responding to the news, the Trump transition team dismissed the assessment by comparing it to flawed intelligence reports in the lead-up to the Iraq war.

"These are the same people that said Saddam Hussein had weapons of mass destruction," the statement said.

October 2016: Questioning intelligence consensus that Russia is to blame. On Oct. 7, the United States intelligence community released a joint public statement saying it was "confident that the Russian government" had directed cyberattacks on American individuals and institutions, including political organizations such as the Democratic National Committee.

Three days after that, during the second presidential debate, Mr. Trump again cast doubt that Russia was responsible — or even that there was a cyberattack in the first place.

"Maybe there is no hacking. But they always blame Russia. And the reason they blame Russia because they think they're trying to tarnish me with Russia," he said.

September 2016: Continuing to cast doubt on Russian meddling. As the official nominees of their parties, Mr. Trump and Hillary Clinton began receiving intelligence reports in early August. On Sept. 22, top Democrats on the House and Senate Intelligence Committees issued a statement saying that they had "concluded that the Russian intelligence agencies are making a serious and concerted effort to influence the U.S. election," based on briefings they had received.

Four days later, during the first presidential debate, Mr. Trump said, "I don't think anybody knows it was Russia that broke into the D.N.C."

He continued: "I mean, it could be Russia, but it could also be China. It could also be lots of other people. It also could be somebody sitting on their bed that weighs 400 pounds, O.K.?"

June 2016: Rejecting the D.N.C. claim that Russian hackers penetrated its files. The Democratic National Committee and a cybersecurity firm said that Russian hackers had obtained a trove of internal campaign emails and political opposition research.

In response, Mr. Trump suggested that the D.N.C. fabricated the story or hacked itself: "We believe it was the D.N.C. that did the 'hacking' as a way to distract from the many issues facing their deeply flawed candidate and failed party leder," he said in a campaign statement on June 15.

He did not mention Russia.

New Revelations Suggest a President Losing Control of His Narrative

BY PETER BAKER | MAY 3, 2018

AS OF LAST WEEK, the American public had been told that President Trump's doctor had certified he would be "the healthiest individual ever elected." That the president was happy with his legal team and would not hire a new lawyer. That he did not know about the $130,000 payment to a former pornographic film actress who claimed to have had an affair with him.

As of this week, it turns out that the statement about his health was not actually from the doctor but had been dictated by Mr. Trump himself. That the president has split with the leaders of his legal team and hired the same new lawyer he had denied recruiting. And that Mr. Trump himself had financed the $130,000 payment intended to buy the silence of the actress known as Stormy Daniels.

Even in the current political environment that some derisively call the post-truth world, the past few days have offered a head-spinning series of revelations that conflicted with the version of events Mr. Trump and his associates had previously provided. Whether called lies or misstatements, Mr. Trump's history of falsehoods has been extensively documented, but the string of factual distortions that came to light this week could come back to haunt him.

The shifting statements also illustrated starkly why some of the president's lawyers have urged him not to submit to an interview by the special counsel, Robert S. Mueller III, who is investigating whether Mr. Trump's campaign cooperated with Russia during the 2016 presidential election and whether the president obstructed justice to thwart that investigation. Those lawyers have said Mr. Mueller is setting a perjury trap for Mr. Trump. What they do not say publicly is that they worry the president would be unable to avoid contradicting himself.

Mr. Trump has for years presented selective and creative accounts of his life and businesses — "truthful hyperbole," as he put it in his first book — and at times this habit has gotten him in trouble. Even after being elected president, he paid $25 million to settle lawsuits accusing him of fraud for hoodwinking students who signed up for his now defunct, for-profit Trump University.

As a matter of politics, the latest contradictions may not matter much, at least not yet. The public to some extent has grown accustomed to the factual deviations or written them off as unimportant. Just this week, Mr. Trump surpassed 3,000 false or misleading claims since taking office, according to a running tally by The Washington Post — an average of 6.5 per day.

A poll released this week by NBC News and SurveyMonkey found that 61 percent of Americans had already concluded that the president tells the truth only some of the time or less. But even among the Republicans who question Mr. Trump's honesty, most still support him, according to the survey.

And to be sure, not every misleading statement is equally meaningful. In March, The New York Times reported that Mr. Trump was in discussions to hire Emmet T. Flood, a veteran Washington lawyer.

Mr. Trump reacted angrily. "The Failing New York Times purposely wrote a false story stating that I am unhappy with my legal team on the Russia case and am going to add another lawyer to help out," he wrote on Twitter. "Wrong. I am VERY happy with my lawyers, John Dowd, Ty Cobb and Jay Sekulow." Mr. Dowd resigned 11 days later. Mr. Cobb announced his resignation this week. He will be replaced by Mr. Flood.

Under the unforgiving glare of federal prosecutors, however, misrepresentations carry far greater jeopardy. In nearly a year on the case, Mr. Mueller has shown that he is more than willing to charge associates of Mr. Trump with lying to investigators; independent lawyers have said it would be reckless for the president's lawyers to allow him to be interviewed. Even supporters who maintain that Mr. Trump is essentially a truth teller acknowledge that he can be loose with details.

For Mr. Trump, it is about creating a narrative that suits his desired image, and dictating the terms of his own life — in media coverage, in his business, in politics, even in his medical care. But he now risks losing his grip on the story line he has long sought to control, in part because of his own treatment of associates like his doctor and the lawyer who paid the porn star.

This week's revelation about the true origin of the doctor's statement may not have surprised many. When Dr. Harold N. Bornstein released a letter in December 2015 saying that Mr. Trump would be "the healthiest individual ever elected to the presidency," few believed it was authentic. It contained the exact language about "strength and stamina" that the candidate often used to describe himself.

Dr. Bornstein confirmed this week that Mr. Trump had dictated the letter, a disclosure that stemmed from his own split with the president. After he told The Times last year that Mr. Trump used hair-loss medicine, the president was angry and embarrassed, according to aides. Mr. Trump, who often calculates the risks of angering people who know intimate details about him, did not express his frustration publicly. But he sent aides to seize his medical records from Dr. Bornstein, who felt burned enough by the incident to break his silence.

Likewise, Mr. Trump has to worry about whether his brusque treatment of his longtime lawyer, Michael D. Cohen, might come back to hurt him. Mr. Cohen, now facing an investigation by federal prosecutors in New York, originally said that he made the $130,000 payment to the porn actress, whose given name is Stephanie Clifford, from a home equity line of credit and that he was not reimbursed by the Trump Organization or campaign.

Mr. Trump, asked by reporters on Air Force One last month whether he knew about the payment to Ms. Clifford, said "no." He likewise said he did not know where the money came from.

But in an interview on Fox News on Wednesday night, Rudolph W. Giuliani, the former New York mayor now serving as a lawyer for the president, said Mr. Trump had reimbursed Mr. Cohen for the money.

In a follow-up interview on Thursday morning, Mr. Giuliani said Mr. Trump did not actually learn the specifics until recently. "He didn't know the details of this until we knew the details of this, which was a couple weeks ago," Mr. Giuliani said. "Maybe not even a couple — maybe 10 days ago."

Mr. Giuliani seemed less concerned with explaining Mr. Trump's previous denial than with emphasizing that it was the candidate's personal money and therefore could not be a violation of campaign finance law. He said the payment to Ms. Clifford as part of a nondisclosure agreement was made in October 2016 only to protect Mr. Trump's family from a false allegation, not to influence the election less than two weeks later.

While others might think paying $130,000 to someone who was making a false allegation was hard to fathom, for a wealthy man like Mr. Trump it was not quite "pocket change, but it's pretty close to it," Mr. Giuliani said.

"When Cohen heard $130,000, he said: 'My God, this is cheap — they come cheap. Let me get the thing signed up and signed off,' " Mr. Giuliani added.

The disclosure prompted a message of vindication from Ms. Clifford's lawyer, Michael Avenatti. "We predicted months ago that it would be proven that the American people had been lied to as to the $130k payment and what Mr. Trump knew, when he knew it and what he did in connection with it," he wrote on Twitter. "Every American, regardless of their politics, should be outraged by what we have now learned. Mr. Trump stood on AF1 and blatantly lied."

In his Wednesday night interview, Mr. Giuliani also offered a different reason for Mr. Trump's decision to fire James B. Comey as F.B.I. director last year. When Mr. Trump first announced the dismissal, he explained it by saying that Mr. Comey was "not able to effectively lead the bureau" and cited memos criticizing his handling of the investigation into Hillary Clinton's email server. The next day, Mr. Trump told Lester Holt on NBC News that he would have fired Mr.

Comey regardless of the memos and that he had the Russia investigation on his mind.

On Fox News, Mr. Giuliani attributed the decision to Mr. Comey's refusal to publicly exonerate Mr. Trump in the Russia investigation. "He fired Comey because Comey would not, among other things, say that he wasn't a target of the investigation," Mr. Giuliani said. Since then, Mr. Mueller's office has told the White House that Mr. Trump is a subject, though not a target, of the investigation.

Mr. Giuliani told The Times that he had consulted with Mr. Trump before and after making the revelation about the $130,000 payment on Wednesday night, and the president posted a series of messages on Twitter on Thursday morning that read as if drafted by a lawyer to elaborate.

But some still wondered whether it was an unscripted comment, especially given that it came up almost casually at the end of a long interview with Sean Hannity, the Fox News host. Mr. Giuliani and Mr. Trump have a long and deep relationship. The former mayor has the president's ear — and understands how to communicate with him — in a way that few others do.

Still, Mr. Giuliani is a former big city mayor accustomed to being an executive, and his ability to simply carry out orders without adding his own flair has always been in question.

Either way, the last few days have shown that Mr. Trump's narrative is now at least in part in the hands of others — his lawyers, his friends, his doctor, his accuser's lawyer, even his investigators. And for a man who prefers to craft his own story line, that is not a comfortable situation.

MAGGIE HABERMAN CONTRIBUTED REPORTING.

Where Trump Succeeded

OPINION | BY CHARLES M. BLOW | JUNE 3, 2018

IN ONE WAY, Donald Trump's presidency has been a raging success: He stole a political party.

Among most of the people who we used to call Republicans, among the people who like Trump or at least loathe the things that Trump loathes, Trump is not a disappointment but a deity.

As the former House speaker, John Boehner, said Thursday at a political event in Michigan: "There is no Republican Party. There's a Trump party. The Republican Party is kind of taking a nap somewhere."

No sir, the Republican Party as you knew it — and I knew it — is in a Trump-induced coma. As Trump dragged down your party, Republican voters cheered, and your so-called leaders have cowered.

Congressmen have shielded and protected him, excused and accepted him. The party as a whole — or at least the vast majority of it — has turned its back on much of what it once held dear, and heretofore adhered to: a common sense of morality, ethics and norms or propriety.

To be clear, much of what Trump has surfaced among Republicans has always been there — sexism, racism, xenophobia, anti-immigrant hysteria — but Trump has elevated it, venerated it and branded it. This is the Trumpublican Party, a party reborn in Trump's own image, one existing to worship him with blind allegiance and follow him with mindless obeisance.

For instance, Trump has a long history of womanizing. Republicans shrugged. He bragged on tape about assaulting women. Republicans shrugged. He has now been exposed as having paid a porn star for her silence about an alleged affair, and Republicans have shrugged.

Most of these people, in their misogyny and patriarchy (including the majority of white women voters in America who voted for Trump in 2016) — don't see a problem with the way Trump treats women. An

April Quinnipiac University poll found that two-thirds of Republicans believe that "Trump treats women with the same amount of respect as he treats men."

Furthermore, a YouGov poll from the end of April found that while a majority of Trump voters believe that a woman would probably be elected president during their lifetimes, a majority hoped it wouldn't happen. Trump has attacked people who are black (protesting athletes, immigrants from African countries, President Obama) and brown (Mexicans, Muslims, immigrants coming north) and the Trumpublicans have cheered.

Trump has defended Nazis and has been slow and tentative about criticizing racists. He has invited flaming racist Ted Nugent to the White House. Nugent has called President Obama a piece of human excrement, referred to Jesse Jackson and Al Sharpton's speech in a column as "lisping their ebonic mumbo-jumbo," and wrote in another column, "I'm beginning to wonder if it would have been best had the South won the Civil War."

Trump has pardoned Sheriff Joe Arpaio, who ordered the systematic racial profiling of Latino communities. As the A.C.L.U. put it: "In traffic stops, workplace raids and neighborhood sweeps, Arpaio ordered deputies to target residents solely based on their ethnicity, often detaining people without reasonable suspicion that they were violating any laws that his office was allowed to enforce."

And last week Trump pardoned racist Dinesh D'Souza, who as Slate put it, "has trafficked in racism and homophobia for nearly 30 years, stretching back to his time at Dartmouth in the early years of the Reagan administration, where he edited the right-wing Dartmouth Review. Among other things, he ran an anti-affirmative action article written in a caricature of black vernacular English (titled "Dis Sho Ain't No Jive, Bro")..."

And yet, the same April Quinnipiac poll found that an overwhelming 82 percent of Republicans believe Trump treats people of color with the same amount of respect as he treats white people.

These people were already detached from reality, but Trump helped them to see a new reality, one in which their hatred and bigotry were not abhorrent, but rather markers of the mainstream. They didn't have a problem, the rest of America was the problem.

It is only in that alternate reality, in that other world, that Gallup could report poll results last week that found that three-quarters of Republicans believe that Trump provides strong moral leadership as president.

These are the same Republicans who told Gallup last month that they thought that the ethical standards of the thoroughly unethical Trump administration officials were excellent or good (71 percent) as opposed to not good or poor (27 percent).

I will not say that the pre-Trump Republican Party is dead, because anything can happen in politics, but I will most definitely say that it is grievously ill, on life support and Trump is standing over the motionless body with the power cord in his hand.

For conquering and crippling the Republican Party, Trump will be long remembered, but probably not in the way his supporters hope. I believe he is leading them to ruin.

Trump Calls for Depriving Immigrants Who Illegally Cross Border of Due Process Rights

BY KATIE ROGERS AND SHERYL GAY STOLBERG | JUNE 24, 2018

PRESIDENT TRUMP unleashed an aggressive attack Sunday on unauthorized immigrants and the judicial system that handles them, saying that those who cross into the United States illegally should be sent back immediately without due process or an appearance before a judge.

"We cannot allow all of these people to invade our Country," Mr. Trump tweeted while on the way to his golf course in Virginia. "When somebody comes in, we must immediately, with no Judges or Court Cases, bring them back from where they came."

It was another twist in a head-spinning series of developments on immigration since the administration announced a "zero tolerance" policy two months ago, leading to the separation of children from parents who cross the border illegally and an outcry from Democrats and many Republicans.

Mr. Trump signed an executive order to end the separations last week, but the sudden shifts have led to confusion along the border about how children and parents will be reunited and to turmoil in Congress as the House prepares to vote on a sweeping immigration bill this week.

Still, the president, who has always dug his heels in when criticized, has not backed back down from his hard-line talk, even amid a national outcry over a detainment policy that has resulted in the separation of more than 2,300 children from their families.

He has instead gone on the offensive, complaining to aides about why he could not just create an overarching executive order to solve the problem, according to two people familiar with the deliberations. Aides have had to explain to the president why a comprehensive immigration overhaul is beyond the reach of his executive powers.

And privately, the president has groused that he should not have signed the order undoing separations.

"Our system is a mockery to good immigration policy and Law and Order," Mr. Trump tweeted Sunday, adding, "Our Immigration policy, laughed at all over the world, is very unfair to all of those people who have gone through the system legally and are waiting on line for years! Immigration must be based on merit."

But Mr. Trump's call to ignore due process faced both constitutional questions and dissension from Republicans in Congress, some of whom have insisted that the number of judges be increased so migrant families can have their cases heard more quickly. Federal immigration courts faced a backlog of more than 700,000 cases in May, and cases can take months or years to be heard.

Senator Ted Cruz, Republican of Texas, has proposed doubling the number of judges to roughly 750, while Senator Ron Johnson, Republican of Wisconsin and chairman of the Senate Homeland Security Committee, said Sunday on CNN's "State of the Union" that he believes an additional 225 judges are needed. He noted that only 74 of the current immigration judges are serving at the border.

"We need to increase that," Mr. Johnson said. "The Trump administration is going to try and come up with another 15,000 beds for family units. But none of this is easy."

The House bill up for a vote this week would beef up border security and provide a path to citizenship for the young undocumented immigrants known as Dreamers, while also effectively codifying Mr. Trump's executive order by allowing migrant families to be detained together indefinitely.

Many on Capitol Hill believe legislation is necessary to deal with the order, since it allows indefinite detentions. Under a 1997 consent decree known as the Flores settlement, migrant children can be detained for no more than 20 days, leaving the order's status in court in doubt.

But the president's conflicting statements are complicating legislative efforts, said Senator Jeff Flake, Republican of Arizona.

"It makes it very difficult," Mr. Flake said on ABC's "This Week," continuing, "It's difficult in any event, right, in an election year where the president has decided to have this at the forefront of the Republican election strategy to paint the Democrats as soft on immigration."

He added: "I don't know how in the world we're going to fix this in the short term, given the Flores decision and given the lack of infrastructure, judges to process these claims. It's really a big mess."

Mr. Trump's tweets on Sunday threw new legal questions into the puzzle. Laurence H. Tribe, a constitutional law professor at Harvard, said in an email that the Supreme Court has repeatedly held that "the due process requirements of the Fifth and 14th Amendments apply to all persons, including those in the U.S. unlawfully."

"Trump is making the tyrannical claim that he has the right to serve as prosecutor, judge and jury with respect to all those who enter our country," Mr. Tribe said. "That is a breathtaking assertion of unbounded power — power without any plausible limit."

The Fifth Amendment mandates the due process of law, and the 14th Amendment, in part, expanded due process rights for immigrants, with case law asserting those rights dating back to 1886. But Justice Department lawyers under both Democratic and Republican administrations have argued that noncitizens apprehended at the border lack due process protections, said Adam Cox, a law professor at New York University, and the Supreme Court has never clearly resolved the dispute.

Since Mr. Trump was elected, his administration has been working to expand the terms of a 1996 statute that allows immigration officials to quickly deport undocumented immigrants as well as those whose papers are believed to be fraudulent. The Trump administration has the ability to expand the statute to encompass the entire country and apply it to any noncitizen who has not been in the country for more than two years, Mr. Cox said.

"One of the things that is being considered is an expanded expedited removal to the full statutory limit," he said, adding that "it is already true that a lot of people show up at the border get removed with no access to immigration courts or the judicial process."

Mr. Cox said the president could be reacting to seeing a high number of people held in detention centers claiming they face harm back home. The White House did not immediately respond to a request for comment on whether the president knew the legal ins and outs of his demand.

"Many members of the administration seem to think that the high rate necessarily means a lot of fraud," Mr. Cox said of asylum claims, "so what they could like to do is remove that process."

Attorney General Jeff Sessions, who has made illegal immigration a focus of his career, has moved to back up the president's words with action in recent months. In April, Mr. Sessions announced a "zero tolerance" immigration policy, which set off the mass separation of families that the president sought to end with his executive order last week.

Criminal prosecutions for illegally crossing the southwestern border jumped to 8,298 in April, the month Mr. Sessions announced the zero-tolerance policy, an increase of 30 percent from March, according to data from the Transactional Records Access Clearinghouse, a research institute at Syracuse University. Last week, the Defense Department lent 21 lawyers to the Justice Department to focus on prosecuting a backlog in border crossing cases. And on Sunday, the defense secretary, Jim Mattis, said the Pentagon was looking at using two bases to hold an unknown number of migrants, though he would not comment on their location or whether they would house children.

Omar Jadwat, director of the Immigrants' Rights Project at the American Civil Liberties Union, called the president's demand to dispense with due process illegal. "Any official who has sworn an oath to uphold the Constitution and laws should disavow it unequivocally," he said.

Mr. Trump's call to end due process is not a total surprise — he has alluded to taking similar measures for weeks. While in Las Vegas on Saturday, Mr. Trump told supporters that he thought the immigration system needed fewer judges. Mr. Trump also suggested last week that he opposed adding judges because many of them could be corrupt.

He has long been a critic of immigration judges, saying they were not effective in stopping the flow of people coming into the country, sometimes using incorrect numbers to make his point.

"We have thousands of judges. Do you think other countries have judges?" Mr. Trump said during a round-table discussion in May. "We give them, like, trials. That's the good news. The bad news is, they never show up for the trial. O.K.?"

There are actually fewer than 400 judges dedicated to such work, according to the website PolitiFact.

Mr. Trump also tweeted on Friday that Republicans should "stop wasting their time" on the broad House immigration bill, but Representative Michael McCaul, Republican of Texas and chairman of the House Homeland Security Committee, said on "Fox News Sunday" that he had spoken to the White House, which had assured him that Mr. Trump was "still 100 percent behind us."

Mr. Trump's careening from one extreme to another has been a staple of his campaign and presidency, allowing people to hear what they want in what he says — and leaving his White House to sort through a messy pile of conflicting directives and Congress to grasp for clues about which bills he might support.

The prospects for the House bill are iffy at best; some conservatives are balking at the citizenship provisions, which critics regard as "amnesty." If it fails, Mr. McCaul said the House may be forced to consider a narrower measure — a so-called skinny bill — that would address only the issues surrounding detention of migrant families.

"I think we at a minimum have to deal with the family separation," Mr. McCaul said. "I'm a father of five. I think this is inhumane and I think the pictures that we have seen — that's not the face of America."

KATIE BENNER, MAGGIE HABERMAN AND THOMAS GIBBONS-NEFF CONTRIBUTED REPORTING.

Supreme Court Upholds Trump's Travel Ban, Delivering Endorsement of Presidential Power

BY ADAM LIPTAK AND MICHAEL D. SHEAR | JUNE 26, 2018

WASHINGTON — The Supreme Court on Tuesday upheld President Trump's ban on travel from mostly-Muslim nations, delivering a robust endorsement of Mr. Trump's power to control the flow of immigration into America at a time of political upheaval about the treatment of migrants at the Mexican border.

In a 5-to-4 vote, the court's conservatives said the president's statutory power over immigration was not undermined by his history of incendiary statements about the dangers he said Muslims pose to Americans.

Mr. Trump, who has battled court challenges to the travel ban since the first days of his administration, hailed the decision to uphold his third version of an executive order as a "tremendous victory" and promised to continue using his office to defend the country against terrorism and extremism.

"This ruling is also a moment of profound vindication following months of hysterical commentary from the media and Democratic politicians who refuse to do what it takes to secure our border and our country," the president said in a statement issued by the White House soon after the ruling.

The vindication came even as Mr. Trump is reeling from weeks of controversy over his decision to impose "zero tolerance" at America's southern border, leading to politically searing images of children being separated from their parents as families cross into the United States without proper documentation.

Mr. Trump and his advisers have long argued that presidents are given vast authority to reshape the way America controls its borders. The president's attempts to do that began with the travel ban and continues today with his demand for an end to "catch and release" of illegal immigrants.

In remarks during a meeting with lawmakers on Tuesday, Mr. Trump hailed the court's ruling and vowed to continue fighting for a wall across the Mexican border.

"We have to be tough and we have to be safe and we have to be secure," he said, adding that construction of the border wall "stops the drugs. It stops people we don't want to have."

Writing for the majority, Chief Justice John G. Roberts Jr. said that Mr. Trump had ample statutory authority to make national security judgments in the realm of immigration. And he rejected a constitutional challenge to Mr. Trump's latest executive order on the matter, his third, this one issued as a proclamation in September.

But the court's liberals decried the decision. In a passionate and searing dissent from the bench, Justice Sonia Sotomayor said the decision was no better than Korematsu v. United States, the 1944 decision that endorsed the detention of Japanese-Americans during World War II.

By upholding the travel ban, she said, the court "merely replaces one gravely wrong decision with another."

Critics of the president's travel ban also decried the court's ruling. Senator Robert Menendez, Democrat of New Jersey, wrote that "today is a sad day for American institutions, and for all religious minorities who have ever sought refuge in a land promising freedom."

The Baptist Joint Committee for Religious Liberty said in a statement that "we are deeply disappointed by the Supreme Court's refusal to repudiate policy rooted in animus against Muslims."

Chief Justice Roberts acknowledged that Mr. Trump's had made many statements concerning his desire to impose a "Muslim ban."

"The issue before us is not whether to denounce the statements," the chief justice wrote. "It is instead the significance of those statements in reviewing a presidential directive, neutral on its face, addressing a matter within the core of executive responsibility."

"In doing so," he wrote, "we must consider not only the statements of a particular President, but also the authority of the Presidency itself."

He concluded that the proclamation, viewed in isolation, was neutral and justified by national security concerns. "The proclamation is expressly premised on legitimate purposes: preventing entry of nationals who cannot be adequately vetted and inducing other nations to improve their practices," he wrote.

Even as it upheld the travel ban, the majority took a momentous step. It overruled Korematsu v. United States, the 1944 decision that endorsed the detention of Japanese-Americans during World War II.

But Chief Justice Roberts said Tuesday's decision was very different.

"The forcible relocation of U. S. citizens to concentration camps, solely and explicitly on the basis of race, is objectively unlawful and outside the scope of presidential authority," he wrote. "But it is wholly inapt to liken that morally repugnant order to a facially neutral policy denying certain foreign nationals the privilege of admission."

"The entry suspension is an act that is well within executive authority and could have been taken by any other president — the only question is evaluating the actions of this particular president in promulgating an otherwise valid proclamation," Chief Justice Roberts wrote.

Justices Anthony M. Kennedy, Clarence Thomas, Samuel A. Alito Jr. and Neil M. Gorsuch joined the majority opinion.

Justice Sotomayor lashed out at Mr. Trump, quoting anti-Muslim statements that he made as a candidate and, later, as president. She noted that he called for a "total and complete ban" on Muslims entering the United States and tweeted that "we need a travel ban for certain dangerous countries."

"Let the gravity of those statements sink in," Justice Sotomayor said. "Most of these words were spoken or written by the current president of the United States."

She dismissed the majority's argument that the government made its case that the travel ban is necessary for national security, saying that no matter how much the government tried to "launder" the president's statements, "all of the evidence points in one direction."

Justice Sotomayor accused her colleagues in the majority of "unquestioning acceptance" of the president's national security claims. Justice Ruth Bader Ginsburg joined Justice Sotomayor's dissent.

In a second, milder dissent, Justice Stephen G. Breyer, joined by Justice Elena Kagan, questioned whether the administration could be trusted to enforce what he called "the proclamation's elaborate system of exemptions and waivers."

In a concurrence, Justice Anthony M. Kennedy emphasized the need for religious tolerance.

"The First Amendment prohibits the establishment of religion and promises the free exercise of religion," he wrote. "It is an urgent necessity that officials adhere to these constitutional guarantees and mandates in all their actions, even in the sphere of foreign affairs. An anxious world must know that our government remains committed always to the liberties the Constitution seeks to preserve and protect, so that freedom extends outward, and lasts."

The court's decision, a major statement on presidential power, marked the conclusion of a long-running dispute over Mr. Trump's authority to make good on his campaign promises to secure the nation's borders.

Just a week after he took office, Mr. Trump issued his first travel ban, causing chaos at the nation's airports and starting a cascade of lawsuits and appeals. The first ban, drafted in haste, was promptly blocked by courts around the nation.

A second version, issued two months later, fared little better, although the Supreme Court allowed part of it go into effect last June when it agreed to hear the Trump administration's appeals from court decisions blocking it. But the Supreme Court dismissed those appeals in October after the second ban expired.

In January, the Supreme Court agreed to hear a challenge to Mr. Trump's third and most considered entry ban, issued as a presidential proclamation in September. It initially restricted travel from eight nations, six of them predominantly Muslim — Iran, Libya, Syria, Yemen, Somalia, Chad, Venezuela and North Korea. Chad was later removed from the list.

The restrictions varied in their details, but, for the most part, citizens of the countries were forbidden from emigrating to the United States and many of them are barred from working, studying or vacationing here. In December, the Supreme Court allowed the ban to go into effect while legal challenges moved forward.

Hawaii, several individuals and a Muslim group challenged the latest ban's limits on travel from the predominantly Muslim nations; they did not object to the portions concerning North Korea and Venezuela. They said the latest ban, like the earlier ones, was tainted by religious animus and not adequately justified by national security concerns.

The challengers prevailed before a Federal District Court there and before a three-judge panel of the United States Court of Appeals for the Ninth Circuit, in San Francisco.

The appeals court ruled that Mr. Trump had exceeded the authority Congress had given him over immigration and had violated a part of the immigration laws barring discrimination in the issuance of visas. In a separate decision that was not directly before the justices, the United States Court of Appeals for the Fourth Circuit, in Richmond, Va., blocked the ban on a different ground, saying it violated the Constitution's prohibition of religious discrimination.

Glossary

bankruptcy In business, a federal court procedure that helps businesses pay off or remove debt.

Breitbart The Breitbart News Network, or Breitbart, is a provocative, far-right leaning news website.

Capitol Hill A term for the United States Congress.

caucus A meeting of individuals from the same political party to select candidates running for office.

collusion A secret and often illegal agreement, cooperation or conspiracy.

cyberattack An attempt to damage or gain illegal access to a computer network.

deportation The expulsion of an illegal immigrant from a country.

disavow To deny responsibility for.

electoral college A body of electors that represent the states of the U.S., who cast votes in the presidential election on behalf of their state.

elite A select group of people, considered to be superior to others because of certain talents or privileges.

fake news Fabricated news that is presented as accurate.

far-right A term for the extreme right of a political party, usually based on fascist, racist or reactionary ideologies.

liberal Pertaining to a political party that advocates for individual rights and progressive reform.

meddling To involve oneself, usually without invitation, in a matter that is not one's concern.

national security The protection of a nation, through both the country's national defense and foreign relations.

pundit An expert in a particular field.

racism The belief that race is a determinant of human capacities; the antagonism, discrimination, or prejudice against those of other races.

refugee Someone who has left their country to flee war or natural disaster.

sanction A penalty.

Vladimir Putin The Russian statesman who has served as President of Russia since 2000.

WikiLeaks An international, non-profit organization that disseminates confidential information and documents.

Media Literacy Terms

"Media literacy" refers to the ability to access, understand, critically assess and create media. The following terms are important components of media literacy, and they will help you critically engage with the articles in this title.

angle The aspect of a news story that a journalist focuses on and develops.

attribution The method by which a source is identified or by which facts and information are assigned to the person who provided them.

balance Principle of journalism that both perspectives of an argument should be presented in a fair way.

bias A disposition of prejudice in favor of a certain idea, person or perspective.

byline Name of the writer, usually placed between the headline and the story.

caption Identifying copy for a picture; also called a legend or cutline.

chronological order Method of writing a story presenting the details of the story in the order in which they occurred.

column Type of story that is a regular feature, often on a recurring topic, written by the same journalist, generally known as a columnist.

commentary Type of story that is an expression of opinion on recent events by a journalist generally known as a commentator.

credibility The quality of being trustworthy and believable, said of a journalistic source.

critical review Type of story that describes an event or work of art, such as a theater performance, film, concert, book, restaurant, radio or television program, exhibition or musical piece, and offers critical assessment of its quality and reception.

editorial Article of opinion or interpretation.

fake news A fictional or made-up story presented in the style of a legitimate news story, intended to deceive readers; also commonly used to criticize legitimate news that one dislikes because of its perspective or unfavorable coverage of a subject.

feature story Article designed to entertain as well as to inform.

headline Type, usually 18 point or larger, used to introduce a story.

human interest story Type of story that focuses on individuals and how events or issues affect their life, generally offering a sense of relatability to the reader.

impartiality Principle of journalism that a story should not reflect a journalist's bias and should contain balance.

intention The motive or reason behind something, such as the publication of a news story.

interview story Type of story in which the facts are gathered primarily by interviewing another person or persons.

inverted pyramid Method of writing a story using facts in order of importance, beginning with a lead and then gradually adding paragraphs in order of relevance from most interesting to least interesting.

motive The reason behind something, such as the publication of a news story or a source's perspective on an issue.

news story An article or style of expository writing that reports news, generally in a straightforward fashion and without editorial comment.

op-ed An opinion piece that reflects a prominent journalist's opinion on topic of interest.

paraphrase The summary of an individual's words, with attribution, rather than a direct quotation of their exact words.

plagiarism An attempt to pass another person's work as one's own without attribution.

quotation The use of an individual's exact words indicated by the use of quotation marks and proper attribution.

reliability The quality of being dependable and accurate, said of a journalistic source.

rhetorical device Technique in writing intending to persuade the reader or communicate a message from a certain perspective.

source The origin of the information reported in journalism.

style A distinctive use of language in writing or speech; also a news or publishing organization's rules for consistent use of language with regards to spelling, punctuation, typography and capitalization, usually regimented by a house style guide.

tone A manner of expression in writing or speech.

Media Literacy Questions

1. In "Donald Trump, Real Estate Promoter, Builds Image as He Buys Buildings" (on page 10), Judy Klemesrud directly quotes Donald Trump. What are the strengths of the use of a direct quote as opposed to a paraphrase? What are its weaknesses? Is the subject of an interview always a reliable source?

2. What is the intention of the article "Between Playboy's Pages, a Peek at How a Future Donald Trump Would Campaign" (on page 31)? How effectively does it achieve its intended purpose?

3. "How Donald Trump Keeps Changing His Mind on Abortion, Torture and Banning Muslims" (on page 67) features a photograph. What does this photograph add to the article?

4. Analyze the authors' point of view in "Donald Trump Borrows From Bernie Sanders's Playbook to Woo Democrats" (on page 63) and "How Donald Trump Keeps Changing His Mind on Abortion, Torture and Banning Muslims" (on page 67). Do you think one journalist is more balanced in their reporting than the other? If so, why do you think so?

5. Compare the headlines of "Donald Trump on Protester: 'I'd Like to Punch Him in the Face' " (on page 42) and "Riskiest Political Act of 2016? Protesting at Rallies for Donald Trump" (on page 44). Which is a more compelling headline, and why? How could the less compelling headline be changed to better draw the reader's interest?

6. Does Maggie Haberman demonstrate the journalistic principle of balance or impartiality in her article "Donald Trump's Apology That Wasn't" (on page 95)? If so, how did she do so? If not, what could she have included to make her article more balanced or impartial?

7. What type of story is "The Parent-Child Discussion That So Many Dread: Donald Trump" (on page 57)? Can you identify another article in this collection that is the same type of story?

8. "At Conference, Political Consultants Wonder Where They Went Wrong" (on page 126) features photographs of political consultants and pollsters. What do these photos add to the article?

9. Does "Trump Sexual Misconduct Allegations Repeated by Several Women" (on page 158) use multiple sources? What are the strengths of using multiple sources in a journalistic piece? What are the weaknesses of relying heavily on one source?

10. Compare the headlines of "Donald Trump Rode to Power in the Role of the Common Man" (on page 141) and "When the Leader of the Free World Is An Ugly American" (on page 177). Which is a more compelling headline, and why? How could the less compelling headline be changed to better draw the reader's interest?

Citations

All citations in this list are formatted according to the Modern Language Association's (MLA) style guide.

BOOK CITATION

NEW YORK TIMES EDITORIAL STAFF, THE. *Donald J. Trump.* New York: New York Times Educational Publishing, 2019.

ONLINE ARTICLE CITATIONS

BAKER, PETER. "New Revelations Suggest a President Losing Control of his Narrative." *The New York Times*, 3 May 2018, https://www.nytimes.com/2018/05/03/us/politics/trump-revelations-narrative.html.

BAKER, PETER. "Trump's Meeting With Kim Jong-un Is Another Pledge to Do What Nobody Else Can." *The New York Times*, 8 Mar. 2018, https://www.nytimes.com/2018/03/08/us/politics/trump-meeting-kim-jong-un.html.

BARBARO, MICHAEL. "Between Playboy's Pages, a Peek at How a Future Donald Trump Would Campaign." *The New York Times*, 31 Mar. 2016, https://www.nytimes.com/2016/04/01/us/politics/donald-trump-playboy-interview.html.

BARBARO, MICHAEL. "New York Attorney General Is Investigating Trump's For-Profit School." *The New York Times*, 19 May 2011, https://www.nytimes.com/2011/05/20/nyregion/trumps-for-profit-school-said-to-be-under-investigation.html.

BLOW, CHARLES M. "Where Trump Succeeded." *The New York Times*, 3 June 2018, https://www.nytimes.com/2018/06/03/opinion/trump-republican-party.html.

BURNS, ALEXANDER. "Donald Trump Rode to Power in the Role of the Common Man." *The New York Times*, 9 Nov. 2016, https://www.nytimes.com/2016/11/09/us/politics/donald-trump-wins.html.

CONFESSORE, NICHOLAS. "For Whites Sensing Decline, Donald Trump Unleashes Words of Resistance." *The New York Times*, 13 Jul. 2016, https://

www.nytimes.com/2016/07/14/us/politics/donald-trump-white-identity.html.

CORASANITI, NICK, AND MAGGIE HABERMAN. "Donald Trump on Protester: 'I'd Like to Punch Him in the Face.' " *The New York Times*, 23 Feb. 2016, https://www.nytimes.com/politics/first-draft/2016/02/23/donald-trump-on-protester-id-like-to-punch-him-in-the-face/.

DAVIS, JULIE HIRSCHFIELD, ET AL. "Firings and Discord Put Trump Transition Team in a State of Disarray." *The New York Times*, 15 Nov. 2016, https://www.nytimes.com/2016/11/16/us/politics/trump-transition.html.

FISHER, MAX. "Uncertainty Over Donald Trump's Foreign Policy Risks Global Instability." *The New York Times*, 9 Nov. 2016, https://www.nytimes.com/2016/11/10/world/americas/donald-trump-foreign-policy.html.

FLEGENHEIMER, MATT AND MICHAEL BARBARO. "Donald Trump is Elected President in Stunning Repudiation of the Establishment." *The New York Times*, 9 Nov. 2016, https://www.nytimes.com/2016/11/09/us/politics/hillary-clinton-donald-trump-president.html.

HABERMAN, MAGGIE. "Donald Trump's Apology That Wasn't." *The New York Times*, 8 Oct. 2016, https://www.nytimes.com/2016/10/08/us/politics/donald-trump-apology.html.

HABERMAN, MAGGIE, AND JONATHAN MARTIN. "Donald Trump Scraps the Usual Campaign Playbook, Including TV Ads." *The New York Times*, 24 Dec. 2015, https://www.nytimes.com/2015/12/25/us/politics/donald-trump-scraps-the-usual-campaign-playbook-including-tv-ads.html.

HARWOOD, JOHN. "Imagining Trump Going the Distance." *The New York Times*, 1 Jan. 2016, https://www.nytimes.com/2016/01/13/us/politics/imagining-trump-going-the-distance.html.

HIGGENS, ANDREW, ET AL. "Inside a Fake News Sausage Factory: 'This Is All About Income.' " *The New York Times*, 25 Nov. 2016, https://www.nytimes.com/2016/11/25/world/europe/fake-news-donald-trump-hillary-clinton-georgia.html.

HULSE, CARL. "Once Again, Push for Gun Control Collides With Political Reality." *The New York Times*, 28 Feb. 2018, https://www.nytimes.com/2018/02/28/us/politics/senate-gun-control-nra.html.

HULSE, CARL. "Suddenly, the G.O.P. Remembers All Its Doubts on Trump." *The New York Times*, 7 Mar. 2018, https://www.nytimes.com/2018/03/07/us/politics/republicans-worries-trump.html.

KLEMSRUD, JUDY. "Donald Trump, Real Estate Promoter, Builds Image as He Buys Buildings." *The New York Times*, 1 Nov. 1976, https://www.nytimes.com/1976/11/01/archives/donald-trump-real-estate-promoter-builds-image-as-he-buys-buildings.html.

LIPTAK, ADAM, AND MICHAEL D. SHEAR. "Supreme Court Upholds Trump's Travel Ban, Delivering Endorsement of Presidential Power." *The New York Times*, 26 June 2018, https://www.nytimes.com/2018/06/26/us/politics/supreme-court-trump-travel-ban.html.

LYALL, SARAH. "The Parent-Child Discussion That So Many Dread: Donald Trump." *The New York Times*, 10 Mar. 2016, https://www.nytimes.com/2016/03/11/us/politics/donald-trump-talking-to-your-kids.html.

MAHLER, JONATHAN. "Donald Trump's Message Resonates With White Supremacists." *The New York Times*, 29 Feb. 2016, https://www.nytimes.com/2016/03/01/us/politics/donald-trump-supremacists.html.

MEANEY, THOMAS, AND STEPHEN WERTHEIM. "When the Leader of the Free World Is an Ugly American." *The New York Times*, 9 Mar. 2018, https://www.nytimes.com/2018/03/09/opinion/sunday/donald-trump-foreign-policy.html.

MEDINA, JENNIFER. "Trump's Immigration Order Expands the Definition of 'Criminal.'" *The New York Times*, 26 Jan. 2017, https://www.nytimes.com/2017/01/26/us/trump-immigration-deportation.html.

MOORE, STEPHEN. "It's Trump's Economy Now." *The New York Times*, 28 Jan. 2018, https://www.nytimes.com/2018/01/28/opinion/trump-economy-credit.html.

THE NEW YORK TIMES. "Across the World, Shock and Uncertainty at Trump's Victory." *The New York Times*, 9 Nov. 2016, https://www.nytimes.com/2016/11/09/world/europe/global-reaction-us-presidential-election-donald-trump.html.

THE NEW YORK TIMES. "6 Highlights From Trump's News Conference." *The New York Times*, 12 June 2018, https://www.nytimes.com/2018/06/12/world/asia/trump-summit-transcript.html.

O'BRIEN, TIMOTHY L., AND ERIC DASH. "The Midas Touch, With Spin on It." *The New York Times*, 8 Sept. 2004, http://www.nytimes.com/2004/09/08/business/the-midas-touch-with-spin-on-it.html.

PARKER, ASHLEY. "Riskiest Political Act of 2016? Protesting at Rallies for Donald Trump." *The New York Times*, 10 Mar. 2016, https://www.nytimes.com/2016/03/11/us/politics/riskiest-political-act-of-2016-protesting-at-rallies-for-donald-trump.html.

PARKER, ASHLEY, AND JONATHAN MARTIN. "Donald Trump Borrows From Bernie Sanders's Playbook to Woo Democrats." *The New York Times*, 17 May 2016, https://www.nytimes.com/2016/05/18/us/politics/donald-trump-bernie-sanders-campaign.html.

PETERS, JEREMY W. "Donald Trump Keeps Distance in G.O.P. Platform Fight on Gay Rights." *The New York Times*, 10 Jul. 2016, https://www.nytimes.com/2016/07/11/us/politics/donald-trump-republican-party.html.

QIU, LINDA. "How Trump Has Split With His Administration on Russian Meddling." *The New York Times*, 16 Mar. 2018, https://www.nytimes.com/2018/03/16/us/politics/trump-russia-administration-fact-check.html.

RAPPEPORT, ALAN, AND MAGGIE HABERMAN. "How Donald Trump Keeps Changing His Mind on Abortion, Torture and Banning Muslims." *The New York Times*, 29 Jun. 2016, https://www.nytimes.com/2016/06/30/us/politics/donald-trump-flip-flop.html.

ROGERS, KATIE, AND SHERYL GAY STOLBERG. "Trump Calls for Depriving Immigrants Who Illegally Cross Border of Due Process Rights." *The New York Times*, 24 June 2018, https://www.nytimes.com/2018/06/24/us/politics/trump-immigration-judges-due-process.html.

SANGER, DAVID E. AND CHARLIE SAVAGE. "U.S. Says Russia Directed Hacks to Influence Elections." *The New York Times*, 7 Oct. 2016, https://www.nytimes.com/2016/10/08/us/politics/us-formally-accuses-russia-of-stealing-dnc-emails.html.

SAUL, STEPHANIE. "Trump University's Checkered Past Haunting Candidate." *The New York Times*, 26 Feb. 2016, https://www.nytimes.com/2016/02/27/us/donald-trump-marco-rubio-trump-university.html.

SHEAR, MICHAEL D. "Presidential Election Live: Donald Trump's Victory." *The New York Times*, 8 Nov. 2016, https://www.nytimes.com/2016/11/08/us/politics/election-live.html.

SHEAR, MICHAEL D. "Trump Bars Refugees and Citizens of 7 Muslim Countries." *The New York Times*, 27 Jan. 2017, https://www.nytimes.com/2017/01/27/us/politics/trump-syrian-refugees.html.

SHEAR, MICHAEL D. "Trump Sexual Misconduct Accusations Repeated by Several Women." *The New York Times*, 11 Dec. 2017, https://www.nytimes.com/2017/12/11/us/politics/trump-accused-sexual-misconduct.html.

SHEAR, MICHAEL D., ET AL. "Critics See Stephen Bannon, Trump's Pick for Strategist, as Voice of Racism." *The New York Times*, 14 Nov. 2016, https://www.nytimes.com/2016/11/15/us/politics/donald-trump-presidency.html.

STEINHAUER, JENNIFER. "G.O.P. Legislators Face New Pressure to Decide: Can They Get Behind Trump?" *The New York Times*, 29 Feb. 2016, https://www.nytimes.com/2016/03/01/us/politics/gop-legislators-face-new-pressure-to-decide-can-they-get-behind-trump.html.

THRUSH, GLENN, AND MAGGIE HABERMAN. "Trump Is Criticized for Not Calling Out White Supremacists." *The New York Times*, 12 Aug. 2017, https://www.nytimes.com/2017/08/12/us/trump-charlottesville-protest-nationalist-riot.html.

TURKEWITZ, JULIE. "At Conference, Political Consultants Wonder Where They Went Wrong." *The New York Times*, 14 Nov. 2016, https://www.nytimes.com/2016/11/15/us/at-conference-political-consultants-wonder-where-they-went-wrong.html.

Index